The Christmas MOSAIC II

Edited by Dr. Cassundra White-Elliott

This book contains works of both non-fiction and fiction. In the cases of fictional writings, the stories may have been fashioned after true stories but are not exact retellings.

CLF Publishing, LLC.
9161 Sierra Ave, Ste. 203C
Fontana, CA 92335
www.clfpublishing.org

ISBN # 978-1-945102-25-7

Printed in the United States of America.

Dedications

This book is dedicated to all aspiring writers who were told they couldn't make it in the field of writing or who may have been too scared to move forward because of the fear of failure.

The fourteen authors, whose stories are included within, are proof that you can be successful and your dreams can be a reality.

So, I invite you to pursue your own writing and be the success you know you are.

C. White-Elliott

Dr. Cassundra White-Elliott

Acknowledgements

I acknowledge all the participants in this project, who helped to see it from its stages of inception to its complete fruition.

May your success be plentiful, as you continue to pursue your educational and writing endeavors. I look forward to working with each of you individually, collectively, or both, in the near future.

Much love and appreciation,

C. White-Elliott

Dr. Cassundra White-Elliott

Table of Contents

A White Christmas

Mary Andrews

"Be kind, for everyone you meet is fighting a

battle you know nothing about."

Ian Maclaren

My family was the normal "open one present on Christmas Eve" type of folks. We didn't frost a certain number of cookies every year for Santa when he came sliding down the incredibly narrow brick structure that was our chimney. We also didn't invest much time in knitted sweaters and singing carols to the neighbors on a drastically cold, very bitter Christmas Eve night. No, our traditions were simple, and none of them were worth bragging about. The only thing that was followed to a strict regimen every year was that all the children had to be home two days before Christmas day. I had yet to have a Christmas when even one person was absent.

My two older siblings, Sierra and Mikey, lived about halfway across the country from us. They preferred the world of buildings and busy streets, while my mom enjoyed neighborhood barbeques and the serenity of large backyards that were located in Kansas. No matter what though, Sierra and Mikey were there to enjoy the holiday with us, despite what it meant passing up back in New York. Truthfully, I wasn't sure how they did it. Holiday traffic is like rush hour on an unworldly level.

Sierra was twenty-two and a soon-to-be lawyer. While my mom didn't brag about our Christmas traditions, having a future lawyer in the family was a popular conversation-starter for her. One time, when we were in line at the food market, I heard her slip to the employee, who was bagging our groceries, that if he ever was in a legal matter, my sister, the *lawyer*, was the one for the job. It didn't even matter that she was still in school. In my mom's eyes, it was a sealed deal.

As for Mikey, he was more of the wild child. My brother grew up with a thing for drawing. Some of the crayon marks he made when he was four still color the upstairs hallway of our house. He went on to enhance his talent as a painter, and yeah, he could paint. He was accepted to some of the most sought-after art schools out there, but he didn't go to any of them. Instead, at the age of twenty, he took up a job at a tattoo shop in Manhattan. Of course, that didn't stop him from being my father's favorite and only son.

Besides Mikey and my father, the rest of the house was made up of females. There was my mother, Sierra, me, and my ten-year-old cousin,

Ellie. Ellie had been living with us since she was a baby after her mother claimed she wasn't ready for the role of motherhood. Ellie is like another sibling to us, and no one treats her any differently just because she is technically our cousin.

That leaves me, Avery. I'm the second youngest at the age of sixteen. There isn't anything exciting about me compared to my siblings. I like singing classic songs and reading good books. My parents call me the sarcastic child, and I can't disagree. I did have a little bit of a mouth on me.

Besides my three siblings and my parents, the only other family that came over every Christmas was Mikey's long-term girlfriend. He met her when he was in eighth grade and she was in seventh. She had been to our small, holiday get-togethers since they started dating during Mikey's freshman year of high school. Nina was part of the family at that point, and soon, we'd welcome two more additions to the holiday parties.

Nina was five months pregnant with twin boys. When my family found out over a three-hour Facetime with the expecting couple, I thought my mom was going to hop onto a plane and fly to Manhattan just to cry in happiness with Nina. That was three months ago, and that would be the first time we were going to be seeing Nina in person since she had become pregnant. The best part was that Mikey planned on proposing to her on Christmas Eve, and everyone had been threatened by Mikey to keep it a secret from the soon-to-be mother and bride.

I remember my mother telling me how excited she was that our little family traditions would be growing and becoming even more unique, but it didn't dawn on me how right she had been until the day before Christmas Eve. That day, instead of being at home with my toes curled under a blanket and a worn-out book before me, I was shivering in the back seat of my parents' car. In their haste, they had forgotten to turn on the heat. I could have asked them to turn it on, but my tongue was made of cotton, and I couldn't find it in me to pry open my mouth and request something in the weight of our silence.

Ellie was sitting to the left of me, and Sierra was on the other side. Her forehead was leaning against the cold pane of the window, her breath growing like a cloud on the surface every time she exhaled. She had arrived at our house seven hours before then and told us Mikey and Nina had to catch a later flight because they were behind schedule. Luckily, the couple found a replacement that took off three hours after their original flight, and they had landed about an hour ago.

They were supposed to grab a rental car and drive to our house, which was forty-five minutes from the airport. However, halfway through the drive, Nina began to bleed profusely onto the seat of the rental car. Mikey immediately took her to the closest hospital and called us shortly afterwards.

I had been reading a book in my room when my mom began screaming for us to get dressed, and we were all in the car two minutes later. That's why it was so silent in the car. No one could think of warm small talk that could soothe the knots in everyone's stomachs. With Ellie chewing on her fingernails, my mom tapping the middle console with the pads of her fingertips, and my father's constant need to clear his throat as he drove through the oncoming flurry of snow, I knew everyone was as nervous as I was.

Something was wrong with the twins; that was the only thing I could focus on as I watched with hazy eyes as the scenery outside the car flew past. I could tell from the surrounding area that we were close to the hospital, and that set my nerves on fire. The cream-colored building that was our local hospital rose to greet us as we accelerated towards it. I think my heartbeat was going faster than the car we were in.

By the time we had found a parking spot in the semi-crowded parking lot, a mist of light rain began to cover the world around us. I pulled up the hood on my sweater, trying to cover myself from the shivering I felt, but the fear in my body for the situation presented in front of my family was enough to keep the chill in my bones as I pulled myself from the hunk of rustic metal that was my parents' car.

The second the automatic doors to the building slid open in response to our approach, a wave of warm air rushed over my body. It was enough for the tense set in my muscles to soothe out, and I let out a puff of air. My mother rushed to the front desk to ask for Nina Halmon.

What happened next was pretty much a blur to me, as my parents pushed us through hallways and elevators in search of my brother.

The next thing I knew, my brother was emerging from a hospital room and heading in our direction. He must have heard the hustle and voices of our parents from inside the room. His eyes were red, and he looked sick to his stomach. I heard my mother coo behind me, and before she could grab onto him and never let go, I pushed passed them and went into the room where Nina was.

I heard my brother calling after me, telling me that Nina wasn't awake yet. I didn't listen though. I wanted to see her and know she was okay. I emerged through the doorway, my eyes instantly falling on the form laying on the hospital bed.

Nina's eyes were shut, the blue veins in her eye lids starkly contrasting the unnatural pale tint to her skin. Her arms rested above the sheets, both on either side of her tucked body. My mouth gaped open at the round belly protruding upward. She was bigger than I had expected.

I stood frozen for a second, but the outline of her belly forced me forward until I stood behind the railing of her bed. I looked her over once more, from the knots of her raven hair, down to her covered little feet, and then back up to the smooth skin of her thin limbs. I reached my hand out to her wrist and gently grasped it. Her skin was slightly cold, probably from the temperature at which the room was set.

She did not stir when I held her, and I gently removed my hold, so I could place the flat palm of my hand lightly on the hard surface of her baby bump. After waiting a few breaths, with my hand on the unmoving stomach, I let out a sigh of disappointment. A part of me was hoping that there would be movement from underneath the thick skin, a sign of the twins letting me know they were okay.

Yet there was nothing, and all I could feel was the very subtle rise and fall from Nina's calm breathing. Seeing her in person for the first time in months was enough to make me emotional. In the years that she and my brother had been together, Nina had quickly become one of my closest friends. Even when I was a freshman in high school, and she was my senior, she usually escaped her own friends to hang out with me.

There was a lot we had in common, and having her in my family had become like a blessing. Knowing that my brother and she were going to add to our family was one of the greatest wishes I had wanted since I was in fourth grade. Now that I was there, in a sterilized and cold room where one of my best friends lay motionless, I had never wanted so badly for there to be something close to a Christmas miracle to occur. The grey environment around me gave me a new under-standing of the term "White Christmas."

I rubbed my thumb against the rough blanket that covered the baby bump and leaned down to press my mouth lightly against the skin on the back of my hand.

"Don't worry, my dearest nephews. When you both are born, I'll make sure you never have another Christmas in a hospital."

"Avery," I turned to the voice of my brother, seeing the tears in his eyes. His stare shot to Nina lying in the hospital bed. "She hasn't woken up since we got here. The doctors say it's from the exhaustion and bloodloss."

I took my hand off her belly and walked towards my brother. His lanky form hovered above mine by about a foot, but my arms were long enough that when I stood up on the tips of my toes, I was able to wrap my arms around his neck. I had barely touched his shoulders and pulled him into me before he embraced me fully and started to sob. My eyes squeezed shut at the wrenching sound of his whimpers, and I knew that the situation was what I had prayed it wasn't.

I knew I should pull away and demand to know what was happening to Nina and the babies, but he grasped me hard enough that I knew he was too terrified to say it out loud. I opened my eyes as my family slinked through the door and around us. By the way, my mother had her hand to her mouth, the tears slipping from the corner of her eyes and down her cheeks. It was much worse than what I was expecting.

The crowded room caused the air to turn damp and heavy with sorrow. The stress of it almost made me pull away from Mikey and sprint from the room, but instead, I held onto him harder until the heaving of his body had stopped. When the room was quiet, and I knew I couldn't handle the unknowing future of my nephews, I opened my mouth.

"Mikey…"

"We've lost one, Avery." My heart squeezed tightly, so constricting that it was enough to make me gasp for air at the sudden lack of oxygen. I heard the soft sob of my father from behind me. I pulled away from Mikey, my head crowded with dizzy disbelief.

"How…? I don't understand. How?"

"I don't know the technical terms. I can't even remember what words he used. All I know is that one of the baby's umbilical cords tangled with the other one, and it blocked the other's blood flow. The doctor said this only happens to one percent of babies, Avery, one percent." In the amount of time it took my brother to whimper out the words, my mother had swooped in to tuck her son under her arm protectively.

"Sierra, what's going to happen to the dead baby?" I cleared my throat, trying to keep the tears that were threatening to spill at bay. Ellie's question had my brother hunching farther into the form of our mother, wailing relentlessly. The room grew still again, all of us waiting for him to answer.

Sierra bent down towards Ellie and began to whisper the answer into her ear. I was close enough that I caught the words, my whole body growing cold with the spikes of comprehension. I could see him trying to compose himself during the chaotic loss flowing through him, and I wished to tell him not to worry about it, but someone beat me to it.

"Mikey?" Mikey's cries instantly halted, and he straightened to his full height. Everyone turned to Nina, who was awake and staring at her boyfriend with concerned hazel eyes. I pressed a closed hand to my mouth, my lips quivering to let out a noise of grief.

"Baby, you're awake." Mikey moved over to her small frame, slowly lowering into the chair next to her bed. He took her hand in his own, kissing her hand repeatedly.

"What's going on, Mikey? Why are we here? All I remember is the blood." My nerves were violently trembling, and I felt the oncoming urge to vomit. I involuntarily let out a squeak of sickness. At the time, the room had been silent, and Nina's eyes caught my own.

"Avery, are you okay? You look like you're going to be..." Her sentence was cut off as I swiveled back towards the exit and slammed into the door. The door gave way, and I burst into the hallway. My mother and Nina's worried yelling echoed out behind me. Nonetheless, I couldn't bear to see the look on Nina's face when Mikey told her that one of her babies was dead. All I could hear in my head was the horror in her cries, as she realized she'd have to carry both the babies until birth. Dead and alive.

I ran through the corridors the same way we had come, ignoring the warning from staff to stop running. When I finally found the waiting room on the level I was on, my chest was heaving with the adrenaline pumping through my blood. I was shaking uncontrollably, as I blinked in an attempt to battle the persistent tears. The staff member behind the counter shot me a worried look, but her eyes went back to the computer screen before her.

I shuffled towards an empty chair, roughly throwing myself into the fake leather. I leaned forward, so I could rest my elbows against my knees. My face was in the palm of my hands. I huffed and panted into my skin, trying to calm my fast-paced heart. Besides the continuous tapping of the woman on her keyboard, the only noise I could hear was the rushing of my blood in my ears.

I couldn't fathom what was happening, no matter how hard I tried. I had never dealt with a death, not since I was three years old when my grandmother passed away. This was a loss unlike any I had ever experienced, and I couldn't make out the sorrow in my own chest. So many hours with my mother, talking about setting up our guest bedroom as the babies' temporary room when Nina and Mikey visited. Hearing Nina groan and snap at Mikey over the phone about how her feet hurt, but how the two precious babies made the pain worth it.

All of it, all the talk about when the boys would be born and how they would come down for every Christmas. Now, we were being told we'd be losing one of them? The baby boy still growing in Nina would experience life without his brother. I pushed myself back into the chair, knocking my head into the wall behind me as I looked up at the ceiling as the thought ran through my head.

Nina was going to have to carry both her babies until they were born. The very idea of it brought nausea to my stomach, and I had to fight back the urge to empty my stomach all over again. I moved to stand, so I could go in search of water, when a door to my left slammed open, the knob bouncing off the wall with a resounding slam.

I looked to the person emerging from the hospital room, much in the haste that I had been minutes before. The woman looked like she was in her thirties, her mascara like a path down her cheek bones as she wept. She was sobbing out words repeatedly, all too muddled for me to understand.

She moved passed me and stumbled into a chair a few seats down from my own. I watched from the corner of my eye as she pressed the back of her hand into her right eye, her shoulders moving up and down as she gasped for air. I turned from her, unable to face the pain on her face. My eyes caught movement to my left, and I found myself looking back to the door from which the crying woman had emerged.

In the doorway, stood a small boy, who was no older than six if I had to guess. I looked the small child up and down, and suddenly, I imagined him as one of my nephews. The stinging in the back of my eyes forced me to try and cast my stare somewhere else, but then I noticed that his own eyes were trained on me.

I caught myself staring back him, his clear eyes openly watching me. I looked at him with an irritated type of glare. His staring was beginning to get on my nerves. I felt uncomfortable under his stare, my mouth turning down into a scowl. All I wanted to do was sit here and try and process what was going on, and that kid wouldn't stop staring at me.

Then it got worse, and I watched as he approached me. I stiffened at his approach, not in the mood to talk to anyone at the moment. His feet scuffed against the linoleum tiles as he came closer. I almost told him to go away, that my heart was hurting, and I was going through something he couldn't understand. Instead, I bit my tongue and let him come closer.

When he was so close that I could reach out and touch him, he leaned his mouth down towards my ear. I jerked away from him with a look of disbelief. Surely, this boy wasn't really going to try and tell me something. Couldn't he see I was upset? He lifted up a small, chubby hand and gestured for me to come closer. At that point, I was considering getting up and leaving, but I gave in and leaned towards him. He smiled when I gave him my attention, and he began to speak.

The boy's words tickled my ear as he said them, his hand on my cheek so he could lean forward in hushed tones. With my brows furrowed, I leaned back from him in slight irritation. His words frustrated me, and I wanted to snap at him and tell him he had no right to say that when he didn't know what I was going through. Despite the upset look in my eyes, the boy only smiled. I saw the gap in his teeth where they were still growing in, and I let my anger subside. He was only a child after all. He had no idea what was going on, so how could I judge him for misunderstanding the situation?

I opened my mouth to tell him he was wrong, and that his request wasn't so easy when the boy turned and re-entered the hospital room he had just come out. I let out a breath I didn't realize I had been holding at his sudden exit, relieved that he was gone. As harsh as that sounds, I didn't want to have the company of a child after just being told Mikey was losing one of his own children. It didn't sit well within my queasy stomach.

I leaned back in my seat, the cushion squeaking at my weight as I did so. My eyes fluttered shut, and I tried to ease the headache that was beginning to throb against my temples. I inhaled deeply, trying to clear the fog in my head. The sterilized smell around me was almost enough to make the ache worse. Then, a strange scent for a hospital filled my nostrils. I opened my eyes and flinched back when I realized the boy was in front of me again.

I looked down to comprehend that the smell was the large, red rose the boy held towards me. I looked at him with raised eyebrows, knowing he had taken it from whoever was staying in that hospital room. I stared at him and then the rose, then back at him. What exactly did he want me to do? He shook the stem, causing a few droplets of water from the flower to land on my hands that were clasped in my lap.

I sighed, tired of playing the game that the young boy seemed to have made up. I plucked the rose from his fingers and gave him a tight-lipped smile, hoping it would be enough for him to leave me be. I got my wish, when he gave me another large smile and then turned away. Instead of going into the room like I expected, he turned to the hallway on the opposite side and began to trek down it. Soon enough, he turned the corner, and I lost sight of his small figure.

I peered down at the large rose with a sigh, taking in its soft colors and velvet petals. I wasn't sure how long I stared into the flower, caught up in my own mind, trying to comprehend the environment around me. When I finally came back to reality, I realized the silence around me was due to the lack of sobbing. I turned my eyes on the woman who had been heaving in pain not more than a minute ago. Her swollen, green eyes were on me. My lips parted at the emotion in her irises, a look of agony and astonishment.

"That child..." The crack in her voice was like a baseball bat that shattered the eerie stillness around us. "He gave you the rose?"

I swallowed against the bile in the back of my throat and gave her a slight nod. Her eyes filled with the familiar glassy filter of tears. I watched in confusion while her tongue snaked out of her mouth, so she could wet her cracked lips.

"He's my nephew. Those flowers you're holding belonged to his mother, my sister." The woman's eyes shot to the door from which she and the young boy had both emerged. "We watched her take her last breath thirty minutes ago. The last thing she said to him was that he shouldn't cry, because there are ...."

"Many things to smile for." I whispered the last few phrases the boy had whispered into my ear two minutes ago. *You shouldn't cry, Miss. There are many things to smile for.*

The boy's aunt nodded once in my direction before I saw her place her hands on the armrests on either side of the chair, as she pushed herself up. Her limbs looked weak and shaky, as she turned to go in the direction the boy had disappeared. She did not turn and spare me another glance, nor did I expect to see her or the boy again.

The boy had seen me crying in the waiting room. He had gone back into the room where his mother had just died and gave me her flowers. He smiled, and he told me it was okay to smile, too. The boy had just lost his mother, and he smiled.

I looked at the roses again, knowing the person these flowers belonged to was no longer alive. I fingered the soft surface of the leaf, feeling the dampness on the stem where it had been submerged in a container of water. Tears fell to the petals as I cried, slow droplets carving down my cheek and onto the red flower in my grasp. Through my cloud of tears, I saw the small card attached to the base of a leaf, small and colored in the hue of green. I touched the folded paper with my finger, turning up the front cover to view the ink scribbled onto the rather empty card.

Blinking away my sadness, I re-read the two words on the card.

Merry Christmas.

Slowly, and with a process of consideration, my lips turned up slightly.

I smiled.

About the Author

Mary Andrews currently attends a community college as a recent high school graduate. Her passion for writing has taken her to write many short stories of fiction. Her goals now are to go on to obtain an English degree at a university and explore her options as a writer, so she may continue to share her enthusiasm for the English language with other people. She is very driven in her journey as an aspiring author and wishes to let her readers in on her unusual story ideas and twisted plot lines.

A Rehabilitated Christmas

Kristen Craig

"To thine own self be true."

Shakespeare

A man in all white scrubs walked beside through long halls filled with motivational quotes, such as "One day at a time" and "It works if you work it," Christmas decorations, and pictures of seemingly happy people. My heart was pounding in my chest from the extreme discomfort my body was feeling due to an eighteen-month run with the devil. It was December twentieth and my first day in a substance abuse rehabilitation center for women. The man in white escorted me to an old, rusted chair and told me to wait for a nurse to come and talk to me.

While I waited in that very uncomfortable chair, I looked out the window and noticed bright Christmas lights of all colors around the beaten-up building, almost seeming like it was an attempt to make the place a bit more cheerful for those temporarily residing in it. My nurse, Kensey, a young and beautiful blonde woman, wearing bright red scrubs with little forest green Christmas trees all over it, exclaimed softly as I looked up, "Hello, Kristen. The length of your stay will be thirty days total." My eyes lit up in fear as I realized I would be in rehab, detoxing, rather than spending Christmas with my family.

Heavy tears rolled down my face, and my face warmed up to a bright red from a pale green color. Kensey exclaimed encouragingly, "Oh, honey. It's okay. Everyone here at Mountainside Recovery will do everything to the best of their ability to make sure your stay here is comfortable and enjoyable. I am also a recovering addict, so I know how you're feeling." Somehow that made me feel a little better and less alone. She helped me out of my chair and took me to the pharmacy, which was decorated entirely of Christmas trees, candy canes, mistletoe, and a big beautiful wreath right on the bottom-center of the counter, to see what I was prescribed to help me with the withdrawals I was suffering through.

There was a man behind the counter with the biggest, whitest smile I had ever seen, and he was wearing plain white scrubs just like the man who I walked with before. He searched my name in his database and reached out to hand me my medication and instantly, without even taking it, I began to feel better. Kensey was glad to see I was feeling a bit better and walked me to my room. As we walked through the door to the bedroom, I noticed there was a second bed next to mine. I asked,

"Will I be sharing a room? I've never done that before." She nodded assuringly and said, "Yes, your roommate's name is Emilee. She's around your age, and I'm sure you two will get along just fine." Emilee came out of the bathroom in the room wearing a onesie decorated in little snowmen and snowballs. She had the happiest smile and brightest eyes I had ever seen. "Hi. I'm Emilee!" the girl said very excitedly. From that moment forward, for some reason, I felt as though I belonged there.

The same day, Emilee introduced me to all the women that were residing in the house with us. There were four of them: Carla, Jen, Rochelle, and Chelsea. Carla and Rochelle were two older women who had been in multiple rehabs before but never for an extended amount of time. Jen and Chelsea were young girls, in their twenties, who suffered from sexual assault trauma and battled with drug and alcohol addiction. All the girls were very nice and showed me around inside the building as it snowed outside. I looked through one of the windows and said in a soft tone, "I honestly have never seen snow in person before." And all the girls looked at me like I was insane.

They were all from different states, so they had experienced it before, and it wasn't a big deal to them. Emilee giggled and said, "It's okay. In Ohio, we don't have a lot of mountains. I was shocked when I saw them here." She always said something that made me feel better. Finally, Emilee and I went to our room and lay in our beds. "Thank you for making me feel so welcome. I felt really lost and hopeless when I walked through those doors," I said to her. "We're all worthy of love and understanding, especially during Christmas time," she responded. Then, I drifted off into a deep sleep.

Five days went by, and I woke up to a loud squealing sound coming from Emilee. I was so lethargic and groggy that I could not make out what she was saying until she got in my face and screamed, "It's Christmas. It's Christmas!" I couldn't understand why she was so excited to be in rehab on Christmas but then realized she was happy because she wasn't alone. For the first time, she was with someone who understood her and felt the same pain she had suffered from while battling her addiction. I smiled to her and said, "You know, you make my heart feel whole again."

Even though we weren't blood related, I felt a bond with her like she was my sister. I felt the same excitement momentarily and just hugged her. She held me so tight I felt as though all my broken pieces were sticking back together. I felt closer to her than I did to anyone in my entire family, and that is why that Christmas was one of the most important ones to me. I detoxed through a bad pain killer addiction, realized there is more to live for than drug use, and found in the most unlikely of places what true friendship and acceptance is. I went home twenty-four days later feeling like a new person all together.

About the Author

Kristen Elizabeth Craig is a twenty-one year old recovering addict born and raised in Riverside, California. She began her journey of recovery on August 24, 2016 and has remained clean and sober from all mood and mind-altering substances ever since. As time goes by, Kristen has learned how to be more positive, how to love herself, how to be a better person, and how to maintain friendships and relationships like never before. She has an amazing family consisting of two older brothers, two sister-in-laws, and her very supportive parents, John and Karen. Family is very important to her now, because without all the love, support, and acceptance she has received from her loved ones, she would probably still be living in her rock bottom. Her dream one day is to become a substance abuse counselor and spread her experience, strength and hope to all addicts who still suffer. Her message to all is to grow through what you go through and to allow rock bottom to become a solid foundation from which to start over, rather than have it be the end point of a beautiful life.

Little Lolly

Demian Dimmae

A Life Lost

A child lost and all alone, I had no voice

A child forced upon, I had no choice

My mom didn't hear me, nor did she see me

My dad the boogie man, used and abused me

Courage drained from my inner soul

Allowed fear to creep in and take a hold

Leaving behind tattered and torn

A life lost, a life to morn.

Demian Dimmae

It was a cold blistering Christmas Eve in New Jersey. The ground was covered with fresh powdered snow from the two-day snow storm that kept most people buried inside. It seemed no one wanted to venture out, except us kids. Not many cars were on the road. I guess it was because when it got that cold, cars didn't start so well, which meant One Mile Road would be blocked off for sledding.

It was Sissy who called me early that morning to meet up with her and Boobie at the corner candy store. From there, we would walk to Little Lolly's house. Boobie told Sissy that Little Lolly didn't want to go with us. Little Lolly had been acting strangely the last couple of months. She had become very quiet. We knew something was wrong because she started becoming more and more withdrawn and weird acting. We just didn't know what was making her act that way. She would cry or get quiet when we asked her what was wrong. Our plan was to snap her out of it and surprise her by showing up at her house with candy and bribe her to hang out with us like old times. We figured our candy bribe and begging her would make her give in. We knew how much she liked candy. We also knew how competitive she was, and the mere thought of one of us beating her speed race record down One Mile Road would force her to hang out.

I was so excited to see my friends and go sledding after days of being trapped inside the snow-bound house. I had been trapped inside for two days, doing nothing but watching the snow fall. I thought the endless flakes would never end. The only good thing about being trapped inside was I wasn't inside a classroom. School was out for Christmas vacation. Yay!

That morning, I hurried and ate breakfast, got dressed, and dug my sleigh out of the cellar where it had been since last winter. That was the first big snow we kids had been waiting for. It seemed as though it would never come. During the winter season, going sledding with my friends was what I looked forward to. It was the next best thing to opening all my Christmas gifts, and yes, it was finally Christmas Eve.

I hurried off to meet my friends with my paint-chipped sled dragging behind me. When I got there, Boobie was eagerly waiting, and Sissy was not too far behind me. We heard her calling out our names. We began to run towards each other laughing all the way. We gave big hugs, and off we went, each dragging behind us worn but well-maintained sleds. We all eagerly went in to buy Little Lolly's favorite candy; then, off we went to Little Lolly's house. The closer we got we could see Little Lolly in the distance behind the row housing complex next to a field of trees. We wanted to run toward her, but the snow was so deep we were up to our knees. We thought she was on her way to meet and surprise us at the candy store. But, she wasn't moving toward us.

As we edged closer, we saw her standing over a smoking trash can, not moving at all, but frozen solid. We called out to her, but she didn't look our way. We all said together, "She can't hear us." But the closer we got to her, we could see the smoke bellowing from the old rusty trash can that sat next to the old oak tree behind Ms. Ida's row house. We saw Little Lolly staring as the smoke drifted into the gray sky. She stayed frozen as though she were a mannequin in a department store. The look on her face was a mixture of shock and fear as she heard us call out her name. But instead of beckoning us over, she ran away, leaving the three of us to wonder why.

It was unusual for her to do that because we had dubbed ourselves as the Four Musketeers. Sissy, age eleven, was the chubby one; Boobie, age nine, was the baby of the group; I, age ten, was the tall one; and Little Lolly, age eleven, was the short one. We were the best of friends. Everything we did, we did together. We cut our fingers and became blood sisters. We took an oath to always keep each other's secrets and never lie to each other. We knew everything about each other, or so we thought.

So what could be the reason for Little Lolly to run from us? Naturally, we couldn't wait to see what was burning that made her run away. As we began to rush over to the smoldering trash can, we were stopped by Ms. Ida, better known as the town gossip, rushing out her back door while screaming at us, saying we started a fire. Her voice kept getting louder and louder, accusing us of trying to burn her house down. The whole neighborhood was convinced that she did not like kids that much. She brought with her a dish pan of water, dripping all the way. Before we could explain we had nothing to do with the thick dark smoke seeping out the trash can, she threw water on it.

As the smoke settled, she glanced in the trash can, which now was covered with burnt black soot from the smoke. Suddenly, she had the same look on her face as Little Lolly did. She began to back up, while holding her stomach and shaking her head. Her mouth was moving, but only unrecognizable sounds muttered out. She turned to look at us and became frozen as Little Lolly did. Her eyes were big, and her mouth was open, as she turned and stared at the three of us with a horrified look on her face.

I moved back, and my friends gathered close to me. We began asking, "What is wrong? Why are you looking at us like that?" We insisted we did not start the fire. But, she was frozen for a long time, for what seemed like an eternity. I kept fighting back tears. I knew if she told my mom, my mom would believe her. That is what parents did in the 1960's, believed what the old folks said. I looked at Sissy who then was backing up more and more. Boobie began pulling me by the hand in a gesture to go. I noticed her hand was shaking. I didn't budge. I knew if I did, the story Ms. Ida would tell could cause me not to get my Christmas gifts waiting for me under the tree at home.

I was determined to convince her that we had not started the fire and did not know who did. That would have been a lie, but I wasn't going to tell on my blood sister. So, I kept defending against her words, explaining we had nothing to do with the fire. Ms. Ida suddenly snapped out of her daze and interrupted me and said in a low, slow yet stern voice, "What did you kids do?" Boobie, Sissy, and I looked at each other shaking our heads to signify nothing, as we grew more and more frightened. What was running through my mind was what could be in the trashcan that would cause her and Little Lolly to have the same horrified look on their faces.

I couldn't believe what was happening. It was Christmas Eve, and our plan to go sledding on One Mile Road, which was the steepest hill in town, was about to go awry. All the kids were going to be there. We were supposed to be on our way to a good time. But from the way things were going, it didn't look like that was going to happen. I too wanted to run for dear life. But I guess Ms. Ida saw the terror in my eyes and reached to grab my arm. I moved quickly and said, "I don't want you to touch me. I didn't do anything. You're trying to get me in trouble."

My voice grew louder and turned to screaming at her and talking back, causing the others to begin to scream at her until Mr. Reed, in the house next door, came running to our rescue. As he approached us, my friends and I started to tell what was Ms. Ida was trying to accuse us of. Of course nothing we said could be understood with all of us talking at once. It wasn't until Ms. Ida screamed, "Shut up, you bad kids," that we quieted down, still defending ourselves against her accusations. Mr. Reed asked her, "What in Sam Hell is going on, and why are there ashes on the ground?" They had flown out when Ms. Ida threw water in the trashcan.

We began to speak all at once, and Ms. Ida butted in and said we did a horrible thing and he should call the police. He looked at her in amazement and told her kids will be kids, and it should not be a matter for the police. She told him to look in the trashcan. He walked over, peered in, and slowly stepped back. The color seemed to drain from his face, and he told us how horrible we were, and that we were going to jail for what we had done. He made us stand there, us shaking from fear not cold. I couldn't have felt the cold if I wanted to. I was numb from pure fear of going to jail. That made me more afraid than what my mom would do to me.

Mr. Reed told Sissy to go with Ms. Ida to make the calls to the police and our parents. Sissy was crying so hard she could hardly walk. I stood there begging Mr. Reed to listen to us. Boobie tried to go over and look in the trashcan to see what we were being accused of. She must have been thinking the same thing I was. What could be in the trash that would make them go so crazy and call the police? As she was about to look in, he shouted, "Don't you dare! You don't need to look now. You know what you kids did." Ms. Ida had disappeared into the house with Sissy heavily sobbing.

They emerged from the house a few minutes later, with Sissy crying even harder. A dozen or so people came because they heard the police sirens. The closer the police car got to us, I began to cry. I was so scared. Ms. Ida and Mr. Reed signaled for the policeman to come to them. We watched his eyes get big the more they talked. They whispered so softly I couldn't hear a thing. That scared me more than I already was. I thought when the police arrived, we would finally know what we were being accused of burning.

When I saw my mom, I rushed over and threw my arms around her professing our innocence. I was holding her so tightly she was barely able to move. Ms. Ida had Sissy by the hand to prevent her from running away, which she probably would have. She stated that Boobies' parents couldn't be reached, but a message had been left where they worked. Finally, Sissy's dad showed up with an angry and concerned look and immediately began asking questions. Sissy broke away from Ms Ida's grasp, ran, and hid behind him, saying nothing. Boobie was left without anyone, and I signaled for her to come over to me. She eased over as though she was trying not to be seen. But seen we were. We were the targets of all the commotion.

As the policeman beckoned for my mom and Sissy's dad to come over to where Ms. Ida and Mr Reed were hunched over the now smokeless trashcan pointing down, we kids were told to stay behind. While we three blood sisters stood there trying to figure out what Little Lolly had done, we became more and more terrified of the unknown. We looked at each other, and we all seemed to know what we needed to do. When we saw that look on the policeman's face, we knew we had some explaining to do. But what could we explain when didn't have a clue of what they were looking at.

Mom walked towards me and told me to go home. Sissy was told the same thing. Boobie asked if she could go with one of us and was told no. She asked why and was told because the police didn't want us to talk to each other and that her mom left word she was on her way to get her. We each just looked at each other, crying and wondering what was going to happen to us. We didn't have a chance to make a plan if we would tell on Little Lolly. We didn't have chance to make any plans. I guess that was the plan, just not ours. I hoped Sissy and Boobie would do the same thing I knew I was, just tell the truth. That was the only way we wouldn't be blamed for whatever was so frightening in the trashcan.

Mom finally came home and asked me a lot of questions. Soon after, Daddy came home and asked me the same questions, but with much less sweetness. I told them the truth. An hour or so later, after I had been drilled by Mom and Daddy, the police came to my house to question me. My mom and dad were protectively by my side. The policeman had another policeman with him. They both asked me a series of questions, and I had no choice but to tell them the truth. I told them how we saw Little Lolly behind Ms. Ida's house with the tall oak tree next to the field staring at the smoking trashcan, and that she ran when called her. I told them we went over to see what she was staring at, but before we got there, Ms. Ida stopped us and accused us of starting a fire to burn her house down.

They listened, wrote a lot and said they would be in touch with my parents. As soon as they left, I called Boobie and Sissy and found out they told the truth as well, probably because they were told to tell the truth by their parents and were afraid as I was about what would happen if they lied. It wasn't until we went back to school that not just us kids, but all the kids in the neighborhood found out what was burning in the trashcan.

What was burning consumed the whole town's conversations. The gossip was like a dark cloud, a shadow that followed me, my friends, and, I guess, all the kids who lived in that town. The parents were so afraid that one of us would end up doing something so despicable as what they said Little Lolly had done. Who would have guessed Little Lolly had burned her dead premature newborn baby in the trash, so no one would know she had given birth? She might have gotten away with it, if we had not seen her in the far distance, and she had not run away but to us, which made us curious. If she had only ran to meet us, we would have believed whatever she said she was doing and proceeded with our plan to go sledding.

The chain of events would have never happened. Ms. Ida would have never been the wiser. The trash would have been picked up by the dump truck. We would have had a great time that day sledding and doing what we did best, be kids. Surprisingly, nothing happened to Little Lolly. I guess it was a different time and people in a back country small town went unpunished, or so we thought, especially when they felt sorry for what had been happening to Little Lolly.

For years, she had been molested since she was five years old, yet she never said a word to us, or anyone for that matter. However, what she was dealing with explains why she had changed so much in her appearance. Her mother, months later, admitted that she had suspected something, but was in denial. Little Lolly's dad had gotten wind of what Little Lolly had done and disappeared. He was later found and arrested, but the talk continued, and we lost our blood sister when her mom moved and took Little Lolly away. We thought we would see her some place, maybe the next town over, or when shopping in the nearby city, but we never did. Christmas that year was supposed to be the best ever, but it felt more like a Halloween nightmare.

It took months before the towns' people stopped talking about it. In time, it died like most stories did in towns where life was slow, with nothing to do and the highlight was to gossip. That is what we kids thought anyway: that old people worried too much about everyone's business and not enough about their own. If they had not continued to talk for months and months, maybe Little Lolly's mom wouldn't have taken her away. The moral to this true story, for me, is simple: Mind your own business, gossip less, and do the right thing. That's the silver lining to this story.

Merry Christmas to all, and to all a good life!

About the Author

Demian Dimmae writes poetry and short stories about women in various situations. She tries to reach the readers by pulling them in and taking them on an emotional journey. Her literature provides a short glimpse of the ups and downs around drama, trauma, and sometimes the pleasures that women encounter at one time or another. All her literary works are meant to be conversation pieces. Her goal is to open eyes and hearts to allow for healing.

My Christmas Plan

Shawna Echols

"Family is not whose blood is in you;

it's who you love and who loves you."

Jackie Chan

My story begins in the winter of 1930, the day before our first Christmas, in New York City. My family and I are poor Irish immigrants. My parents, Thomas and Cathryn, came to America in search for a better life for our family. My name is George. I am the third of five boys. Thomas is the oldest and thinks he is the most important member of our family. Charlie is the second oldest, and he is away most of the time, working at a textile factory across town, seven days a week. As I already said, I'm George, number three, the number that gets ignored the most. No one pays me much attention unless I've done something wrong. William is number four and is a rambunctious little boy and often gets into a lot of trouble. The baby is Oliver. He's a sickly child and gets a lot of attention from my mom.

My parents said we came to America for a better life. I was hopeful that would happen, but unfortunately, my dad brought many of our problems with him when he brought his bottle of whiskey. My father is a drunk, a mean drunk who hits anything within three feet of him. All of us boys have been within that three feet many times.

We live in the Irish community of Kingsbridge in the Bronx. Our apartment is located at the end of the block, above Smith's Dry Cleaners, on the fifth floor, at the end of the hall in Apartment 315. When you walk into our apartment, the first thing you notice is the smell of chemicals and garbage. It's a small place with a small dining table, a two-burner stove, a sink, an ice box, and a few cabinets. If you look to the left, you will see a small bed in the corner and two mattresses pushed together against the wall. We only have one window above the sink in the kitchen. There is no Christmas tree or lights and no decorations of any kind in our apartment.

Our apartment doesn't have a bathroom of its own, so we have to share the one downstairs with the fifteen other families that live in the building. Tenants are transient here. The only family I have known since we moved here is the Quinns; they live in Apartment 215. They only have three kids, and Mr. Quinn works for the railroad, so he is away most of the time. Mrs. Quinn works with my mother as a seamstress for the dry cleaners downstairs.

As I make my way home from my job of digging ditches to repair the roads, I pay no attention to my frostbitten fingers, the once white snow now grey with dirt, or the store owners who are decorating for Christmas. My thoughts are all consuming. I know the second I walk in the door, my parents are going to wonder what I am doing home so early, and they are going to bombard me with questions. I contemplate how I am going to tell my parents I was fired from my job. I lost my job the day before Christmas Eve. How could someone do that so close to the holiday?

I was hopeful of the thought of being able to buy small Christmas gifts for my family, especially my mother. I had planned to give my mother a beautiful red broach. Digging ditches wasn't going to make me rich, but it was better than nothing. There are so many thoughts going through my head. The one that keeps pushing its way to the front of my mind is, "I hope my father hasn't been drinking too much today." He might take the news pretty well, but there is a slim chance of that seeing as he usually takes his first drink at eight in the morning, and with Christmas Eve being tomorrow, he might have started celebrating early.

Lost in my thoughts, I look up to realize that I have almost missed my building. I stand at the edge of the stairs. My palms are sweaty. And, I begin to feel sick. I start my trek up the three flights of stairs, and with each step, I feel more and more sick, fear growing inside me. I reach the top of the stairs, and I hear yelling coming from the direction of our apartment. Both my brothers and father are home. My feet are beginning to feel heavy, and I feel like my heart is going to come out of my throat.

I'm standing in front of our door. I turn the knob, step inside, and silence washes over the apartment, as all eyes are on me. The events to follow are a little hazy. I remember a lot of yelling, my mother crying, and the beating I took from my father and Thomas. All of their pent up anger and wrath for the many injustices they suffered were now focused on me. My father had a ruthless look in his eyes like he was perfectly capable of murdering his son. I remember at one point during the beating my brother paused to ask me, "What kind of fool manages to lose a job digging ditches?" I just hung my head and prayed for it to end.

Once they were finished, I drug myself to my feet and staggered out the door. I struggled down the stairs to the bathroom. Luckily, no one was there. I unbuttoned my shirt to examine the damage they had done. My entire backside down to my mid thighs was bloodied and bruised. I could barely move.

The next morning, I awoke more stiff and sore than I had ever been from any beating my father had dished out. My mother was calling me to go to the meat market. It was Christmas Eve, and every Christmas the Plunkett family had their traditional beef brisket. Everyone was sitting at the kitchen table and grunted greetings to me as if the events of the night before had never happened. I took the money my mother held out to me and left Apartment Number 315 forever. I had experienced some pretty disappointing Christmases before, but this was the worst one ever.

I never made it to the meat market, and I never made it home for Christmas Eve dinner. I decided in the middle of the beating the night before that I would never go through that again, so I made my Christmas plan. I left my family, my home, my town, with only the clothes on my back. Fortunately for me, the Christmas spirit caused others to offer me candy canes, fruit, and breads. This became my Christmas dinner.

I walked briskly for the remainder of the day until it became dark and cold. I made it to the train station where I slept in a deserted freight car. I was lonely, sad, and scared, but in the background of the train noise, I could hear carolers singing Christmas carols. My last thoughts before I fell asleep was first that my first Christmas in America was not as joyous as I had hoped, and second, this would be the last time Christmas filled with pain and loneliness. I vowed then and there to make future Christmas holidays happy and peaceful.

About the Author

Shawna Echols was born and raised in Southern California. She is a college student studying to become a radiology technician. She enjoys art, reading, writing, photography, and spending time with family. This story is her first published work. "My Christmas Plan" is a story that is very dear to her, and she is excited to share it with you.

The Little Things Are Valuable

Dayana Elizalde Nava

'Look back for the memories and forward for opportunities.''

Dayana Elizalde Nava

In the old west during the 1850s, gusty winds were howling through the town of Charlington. It was almost nine o´clock in the evening, and the winter storm didn´t allow people to walk freely on the streets. That was the worst storm that the town had experienced in decades; civilians had to fight against the wind that pushed them back with every step. Even covering their faces with their arms wasn´t helpful due to the strong winds.

In a matter of minutes, the streets were becoming empty by cause of the weather. Hidden between the people was a nine-year old orphan boy, his tiny hands grabbing his black beret, so it wouldn´t fly away. The kid pulled gently at the clothes of a recently married couple passing by, asking for a piece of bread, but they just gave him a disapproving look and continued on their way. Such actions towards him didn´t affect his feelings because that was normal for him.

The poor orphan´s mother had become depressed after his father´s death three years ago. While the father was alive, he was the only one working. Yet, they were poor. She was overwhelmed by the combination of depression and poverty. Eventually, she passed away. The house was taken by other people, and he started to wander the streets. Everything he had was taken from him.

Then, it was Christmas Eve, and people were gathering with family and friends to celebrate. When the wind got softer, he could see all those kids playing through the windows, wishing he could have the same opportunities as them. The kid continued walking, searching for a place to spend the night. His legs were weak and trembling, and his hunger prevented him from taking another step. Consequently, he fell in a pile of snow in a blind alley. Deeply asleep, he dreamt innocently of having turkey for dinner with his parents and opening gifts near the Christmas tree.

When the weather calmed down, a beautiful white woman with pink cheeks from the cold was passing to visit her husband in the cemetery, but she noticed a green scarf standing out from a pile of snow. Her curiosity guided her towards the scarf, and when she uncovered the face of the boy with her hand, she noticed his fever. She tried to wake him up, but she received no reply. The kid´s clothes were worn and short because of the years he spent without someone´s care. He only had one ripped sock and no shoes.

It was half past ten on Christmas Eve; no doctor was going to be available. The woman decided to carry him to her house; he was light and easy to pick up, which made sense because the young boy was trying to live each day as he could. While walking with him in her arms, she hugged him gently and covered him with her gray trench coat to warm his body.

In her cozy wooden hut, she laid the child on her bed and placed a wet cloth on his forehead to reduce the fever. While waiting for the child to rest, she approached the fireplace, staring at a black and white wallet photo of her husband. The boy instantly recovered his consciousness after feeling a pleasant warmth, turning his head in the direction of the thirty nine-year old woman; he noticed the sad expression on her face and asked in distress, "Is he your husband, Madam?"

She nodded in acknowledgment. The woman moved towards the boy, showing the picture of her spouse. The kid sat on the bed, looking at it carefully and made a confused gesture.

"What´s the matter?" asked the woman.

"It´s just…that he resembles my father, but he and my mom are with God now, and I am happy that they don´t have to suffer anymore."

She stroked his wavy hair and said, "I am pretty sure you were their most precious gift, and they are looking after you from the sky at this precise moment." Her words comforted him, making his big green eyes shine. She stood up, placing her hands on her waist, and said with a decisive attitude, "Well, it is almost Christmas. Let´s cheer up. What about eating some… chicken? Sorry, I don´t have turkey. I know is a tradition."

"Yes, please!" the kid replied elatedly.

After eating, they played hide-and-seek inside the house, which had no doors except for the entrance. Both of them were having fun, in part due to the company of each other. The clock indicated twelve.

"Have a Merry Christmas! Where are you boy?" She said while looking quickly in the rooms. When the woman found him under the bed sheets, she shook his back. She realized the boy wasn´t breathing anymore.

Delicately, the woman arranged the kid properly on the bed and covered him with the white sheets to the height of his chest. The expression of the kid transmitted an inexplicable peace, and his face drew a tender smile. She kneeled beside the bed astonished and a tear ran down her right cheek. She took a deep breath and placed her hands on the bed with her head down prepared to pray.

Suddenly, she sensed warmth in her arms. The woman slowly lifted her head and saw a dazzling light that surrounded her. It was the kid´s soul saying goodbye with a hug, but before leaving he gave her a message: "This was the best Christmas ever. Thanks for your hospitality. Finally, I´m going to reunite with my parents. Also, someone told me that you should continue smiling like you used to do… like today, and says that he loves you. You know who I am talking about. Be strong, Madam," and disappeared.

About the Author

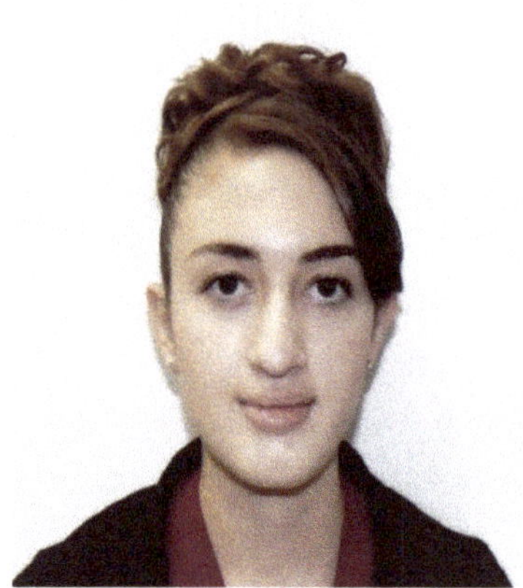

Dayana Elizalde Nava studies chemical engineering at Crafton Hills College. At the age of ten, she published her first short story in Mexico. She has won three medals in spelling bee contests and second place in the science and technology zone competition in the research area. Some of her favorite book genres are mystery, history, fiction, adventure, and fantasy. One of her hobbies is doing crafts.

Christmas Created

Aaron Espinoza

"There's no place you could go where God's love won't find you. No place you could hide that He don't see. No place you could fall that His love couldn't catch you. He sees it all through the eyes of love."

Bethel Music

Christmas is a time of year during winter when hearts are warmed, houses are filled, and joy is in the atmosphere. It is a time where every street is packed with traffic. Every store is hectic with rushes of customers buying gifts for their friends and families. Schools are decorated with holiday cheer, and children create Christmas ornaments. People begin to line their houses with dazzling lights shimmering in the darkness. Christmas trees are on tons of street corners, packed on car tops, and laid in beds of trucks. Red long hats, ending with a fuzzy white ball, begin popping up everywhere. The holiday's main attraction, Santa, also is noticeable, in numerous store promotions and lines waiting to see him in malls across the nation And, let's not forget the countdown to Christmas on television. Surely, it's Christmas time.

However, Christmas had a beginning, years ago. It was a cold winter's night, with winds howling and blowing through the sands of Judea. Sands were sweeping and winds were beautifully singing the beginning of what was to come. The stars all aligned in harmony as one stood out amongst the rest, with creation hovering over its creator. Men from all around followed the star that was glistening amongst the galaxies, leading them to a battered stable where they would all welcome the king, Jesus.

A stable that was nothing more than a pen for animals suddenly became the bed of a king. It was on that night, where everything that was and was yet to come, changed. It was a day that would go down in history, the birth of the Christ himself. It is the story of an ancient tale, known as Christmas. The author of all of time and existence stepped into what He had written, no longer just creating but dwelling in the time He had designed. Christ, the origin of Christmas, there before the start of the beginning of time is a king that is forever robed in wonder and grace.

Not only is there a tale of a big jolly man bringing smiles and gifts to children all over the world but Christmas is a story of Jesus, the one who came to save the world through the gift of salvation. To know that the God of all creation humbly came to the story He wrote, He Himself being the only one to stand true throughout of all of time and history.

Throughout every history story, war, triumph, and trial, He remains. Now, millions celebrate the beginning of this wonder every year in many homes. December is a time to reflect on the goodness of who Jesus is. He is not a myth, but the one whose name echoes throughout eternity.

Decorated trees fill houses with their sweet smell. The nights are cold, and lights shimmer on the corners of rooftops. Nativity sets of the Christmas story are displayed in churches, homes, and even some stores. People buy one another gifts, just like the three wise men that followed the star brought the gifts of gold, frankincense, and myrrh to baby Jesus. Souls sing hymns, reminding the atmosphere of the little baby who was born in a battered stable surrounded by village people with no great significance. It is humility displaced in its greatest form. He is not a king that would boast in himself, but rather a king who would wash the feet of others.

Jesus would go on to preach to the elders in the synagogues, while only being twelve years of age. He is a man who healed the sick, made the lame to walk, and the blind to see. He walked upon water and split masses of seas. He turned water to wine and multiplied loafs of bread and fish to feed to thousands. His wonder does not ending there. He is a man that told the winds and seas to be still, and they obeyed. He is the one who put the image of death upon His frame, taking up the cross that we may live, raising and defeating the grave itself. This king is no ordinary king, not a king that His remains should still be found in the ground. But, He is a king who rose, to ascend back to the heavens He created. He is a man who was completely man and completely God.

Christmas is a season where hearts are warmed and filled with Christmas joy, some knowing why they celebrate Christmas and some not. Over the years, it has become something far from its origins. It is a holiday that is very elaborate with modern day ideas and materials. But, it represents the birth of a baby king in the city of Judea, amongst a cold desert and a dirty stable. It was a night that was seen by few but affected many. It is a season and day that is still celebrated. It's Christmas, a history lesson of a great baby that has forever impacted creation and time. It is the story of the one who created existence, creation, and Christmas itself.

It's not a sound good, feel good tale. But rather, it is the history and the truth, exclusively the truth. However, to depict the characteristics and attributes of the one who created the universe and existence would merely be impossible and fall shy. He is a god of His promise, not speaking in vain or void. Even nature and science follows the sound of His voice. And it is the story of Christmas Created.

About the Author

Aaron Espinoza was born and raised in Highland, California. He is a full-time student at Crafton Hills College. He has completed one year and is working on his second. His major is radiology, and he will be transferring once he completes the classes needed at Crafton. Aaron has been involved in multiple organizations. In high school, he was a part of an award-winning theatre group, serving as part of the tech crew. He then went on to join his high school's Student Body Government, where he served as Social Commissioner. Aside from his high school involvements, Aaron also serves at The Rock Church and World Outreach Center in San Bernardino, California. He is a part of the music ministry and plays the piano. He has completed one year of an internship program with the youth ministry. As a youth ministry intern, Aaron served as a leader for the youth, where he mentored, created graphics and designs, and produced videos. Aaron is currently doing a second year of the internship, while also working at In-N-Out. He is currently a social media department intern at his church. He takes photos for The Rock Church and creates content for the social media platform, reaching thousands weekly. Aaron loves God, family, friends, and life. He loves to travel and see new places. Aaron has a great personality to which many are attracted.

A Christmas Disaster

Savannah Giron

"Our paths may change as life goes along,

but our bond as sisters will remain ever strong."

Six o'clock. I had told my sister over and over again to be ready at six, and now it is fifteen minutes past, and she is barely packing her things. I pace back and forth in front of her bed, frustrated. Leave it to Abby to wait until the last minute to get her stuff together. It's not like I didn't have plans and a schedule to stick to, not that she would care.

My sister's apartment is small, like most studios in New York, and cluttered. There are clothes and junk strewn all over the place. Abs was never one for organization; she liked to live her life one moment at a time, with no regard for anyone else but herself. And try as I might, I could never get her to settle down. She's the older one, but it's always been up to me to stay level headed and take care of her.

"Will you quit pacing already?" Abby asks. "It's giving me a headache." I don't respond for fear that I will say something that will make the seven-hour trip ahead of us even more unbearable that it already will be. I glare at her instead and turn to glance out the window. The snow is dropping quickly, and I am anxious to leave soon.

"I already apologized like a thousand times. Can you stop with the stink eye and just help me?" She shoots me her patented puppy dog eyes look, hoping it will make me forgive her.

I stalk to the bed and grab a shirt, folding it neatly before placing it into her ridiculously oversized suitcase.

"You knew I wanted to leave by six. We can't miss this flight, Abby."

She looks at me again with those stupid puppy dog eyes. "For the last time, I'm sorry. I just need to pack a few more items, and then, we can head for the airport." I give in and help her pack; the more we argue, the later we will be.

When we arrive to the airport, it is a madhouse. There are people everywhere, shouting and yelling. I walk up to a man behind the information desk and ask what is happening.

"All the flights have been delayed. Nothing in or out 'til the weather clears up," he says in a bored voice. Of course, our misfortune is none of his concern.

"Well, for how long? What are we supposed to do? It's Christmas Eve. We have family waiting for us!" My voice grows more shrill with each question, and I can feel myself begin to panic. Abby places a gentle hand on my shoulder, and I turn towards her, anger swelling up inside me.

"This is all your fault!" I shout at her. It's irrational, and I know it, but I can't help but lash out at her.

She withdraws her hand and takes a step back. "How is this my fault? I don't control the weather, Jessica!"

"Had we been here half an hour ago like I'd wanted to be, none of this would be happening. You couldn't just for once in your life be responsible! All I asked was for you to be ready at six, but no, that was obviously too much to ask of you!" I know the words are a mistake, even as I am saying them, but I can't stop. It is as if all of the anger and resentment I have been harboring towards my sister is spilling out now. I have always had to be the responsible one while Abby got to do whatever she wanted with no consequences.

"Woah, Jess! Where is this even coming from?" she asks, with her brow furrowing in confusion.

I ignore her and turn back to the worker, asking what to do now. He tells me to check my bags and go wait at my terminal. That way once the planes have been cleared to fly, we can board. I stalk off to the baggage check, not caring if Abby is even following me. Her heels click behind me, and I know the conversation is not over.

"What the hell was that, Jess? You totally just blew up at me for no reason!"

"No reason?" I ask, exasperated, handing my bags to the lady manning the check-in counter. "I have every reason to be mad at you, Abby. You're so irresponsible!"

"Okay, I get that you're mad. I wasn't packed and ready to go when you arrived, but you didn't need to yell at me like that!"

Grabbing our carry-ons, we both head towards security. I am not even sure what came over me in that moment. Sure, Abby drives me crazy sometimes, but I had never told her that before. As I put my shoes back on, after making it through the security lines, I decide to just tell her how I have been feeling. But I am afraid to hurt her feelings. I have always been the one to protect her, not the other way around. I just can't take it anymore. Just once I wish I could be the one going to her with a problem or to cry about a boy.

Sitting down in the hard seats outside the terminal, I turn to her. This is my chance. "I..." I stop unsure of where to begin. "I just wish you could get it together."

She draws back from me again. I can see the hurt on her face. I backpedal quickly.

"No! That's not what I meant. I'm sorry for blowing up on you. That wasn't cool." I pause again to gather my thoughts. "All of my life it's always been me looking out for you, and I've always had this insane pressure to be perfect and not mess up. And I feel like, just once, I wish we could trade places. That I could be the nonchalant and carefree one. I feel like you're never there for me when I need you, but I'm always expected to drop whatever I'm doing to be there for you. But you're my big sister, Abby, and it's never felt that way." I drop my head into my hands, regretting having opened my mouth.

"I didn't know you felt that way. I'm so sorry, Jess," she says, reaching out to wrap me in a hug. A few tears slip down my face. "I promise I'll try harder to be a better sister to you, okay?"

I look at her and see the hurt on her face still there. She's upset by what I said, but I can see she means what she said. "You promise?" I ask her, still unsure. I don't want to get my hopes up."

"Yes, cross my heart, hope to die. You're my little sister, and I want you to know that I'll always be here for you."

I reach out to hug her, feeling a heavy weight lift off my shoulders. As I sit back and wipe my eyes, a voice comes over the intercom.

"Flight 162 to California now boarding."

"That's us!" Abby exclaims. "California here we come!" Grabbing our stuff, we get in line to board, arms linked, and a smile on my face.

About the Author

Savannah Giron is a college student currently trying to obtain a Bachelor's in English. She hopes to later get a Master's in Business. She enjoys reading and writing in her spare time and is an aspiring author. It is her hope to one day publish a novel.

Christmas Eve

Gage Hopper

The woods are lovely,

Dark and deep,

But I have promises to keep,

And miles to go

Before I sleep,

And miles to go

Before I sleep.

Robert Frost

On a bleak Christmas Eve morning, in the desolate town of Casper, Wyoming, Mayson Brown, an eight-year-old boy living under the presumed care of his grandfather, Travis Brown, lay sprawled across a makeshift bed of yellow-stained pillows and worn blankets splotched with dark crimson. Protruding from beneath the covers rest his frail torso shrouded with a variety of deep purple and vibrant orange bruises further accented by his bleached skin. Awakened by the sound of clattering glass bottles piercing the paper-thin walls of the small home, Mayson stared in complete awe through the partially frosted window at the spectacle given by the heavy, yet light snowflakes gently piling atop the aged spruce immediately outside. A crooked smile instantly parted his gaunt rosy cheeks as a surge of pure excitement struck every nerve throughout his very being, springing the once fragile and aching body to its feet upon the chilled cement floor. Undaunted, only one thought crossed his eager mind: Christmas!

Without hesitation, Mayson raced out of the doorway and down the short and narrow corridor, lined with faded peach and lime striped wallpaper, leading to the living room at the frontal section of the house. Upon exiting the hallway, his nostrils were quickly devoured by the bitter smell of rotting food, alcohol, and cigarette smoke, which constantly clung to the air with a vice grip. Behind the putrid mist, in a tattered rustic recliner chair surrounded by a heap of empty glass beer bottles and half eaten TV dinner trays, sat Travis, an unemployed elderly man with a stocky build, a thick grey beard, and a matching gut, already indulged in his early morning glass of scotch and smoke beside a black iron wood stove.

Still filled with excitement, Mayson raced through the thick blanket of musk and fog straight towards Travis chanting, "It's Christmas Eve. It's Christmas Eve!" Fazed by only thoughts of the imminent holiday, the familiar shout of his grandfather yelling, "Shut up!" immediately brought him back to reality, as he was instantaneously blindsided by a swiftly thrown backhand to the mouth and thrown to the ground. Writhing in pain from not only the initial blow but also scattered ashes leftover from the previously lit cigarette on his cheek, Mayson lay in silence not daring to utter a single word or catch a glimpse of the cold eyes looming above.

Slowly rising from his chair, Travis flicked the remaining butt towards his grandson and said in disgust, "Look what you made me do, Mayson! That was my last cigarette. Now I'll have to get more." While drinking the remaining scotch in the glass, he wobbled toward the front door and began slipping on a pair of heavy black boots and a thick winter jacket over his white tank top stained from previous nights of drinking. Before proceeding out the door, Travis yelled out, "This house better be cleaned before I get back!" without once looking back to see Mayson still whimpering in the same position as when he had fallen.

The door was violently slammed, sending a sub-zero gust of wind and snow spiraling throughout the room. The crisp sound of snow crunching beneath walking feet faded into the distance as Mayson continued to blankly stare at the floor. A single drop of blood fell from the corner of his mouth, gently splashed against his arm. Without making a sound or change in his empty expression, he slowly rose to his feet and began collecting the empty bottles that covered the scratchy circular rug under the recliner. His mind was no longer filled with the joyous and cheerful images of past Christmases shared with his parents, but only recent and dark memories of his grandfather's ruthless drunk rampages. The thought of the events to come created a swarm of butterflies spiraling in Mayson's stomach. Unable to contain the pressure, they were all simultaneously released upon the empty grey cement canvas, creating what could pass as abstract art. Another mess to clean.

Countless hours passed without a second thought as Christmas Eve morning turned to night. Having spent every available minute of daylight cleaning the mess of his grandfather, Mayson lay exhausted and fatigued once again on his makeshift bed. Fading into his own mind, he began to recall distant memories of his past life with his parents. He dreamt of the anticipation he felt waking up on previous Christmas mornings. He had the innocent sparkle in his eyes you would expect any child to have upon waking up to the thought of Santa delivering presents to each home.

Still dressed in his camouflage dinosaur pajamas, he would race across the soft brown carpet of the hallway headed straight toward his parents' bedroom shouting "It's Christmas! It's Christmas!" Not waiting for them to fully rise from their bed, Mayson would joyously leap for the dark oak railing trailing down the half-spiraled staircase lined with pure white lights and golden streamers. Upon reaching the bottom step, his face would light up with so much delight it matched the radiance of the giant star placed atop the lavishly green spruce tree, which was gently decorated with a variety of colored ornaments and lights.

Under the tree rested dozens of neatly wrapped presents blanketing a thick circular velvet rug laced in green and gold. Mayson's parents would watch him with soft smiles at the top of the staircase, as he eagerly tore through each gift signed with his name. Nearing the final present, Mayson's father would jingle his car keys to gain his attention and say, "I think it's time to get your real present, son."

Overjoyed with the idea of possible gifts, he sprinted for the four-doored silver sedan and waited patiently in the back seat prepared to go. As his father entered the car, he violently slammed the door shut, but Mayson didn't mind. Moments later, a soft-scented perfume caressed his nostrils as his mother gently sat in front of him in the passenger seat. The once sweet aroma gave off a familiar bitter and musty sting of alcohol and cigarettes. The smell grew thicker by the second and weighed heavily upon Mason's chest. His lungs caught fire as he began gasping for air but to no avail.

Viciously awakened, he felt the tireless icy grip of his grandfather's hands crushing his throat and caught a glimpse of the cold eyes that pierced his own countless times. Unable to act, he felt the freezing hands disappear and the fire within his lungs dissipate. He no longer felt the pain of the endless trail of bruises covering his body. As everything faded to black, he reemerged in the back seat of the silver sedan directly behind his mother. The sweet aroma of perfume filled his nose once again. That was the Christmas he had longed for.

About the Author

Gage Hopper was born in California in 1998. Shortly after, under the care of a single father, he and his family moved to a rural town in Montana where he spent the majority of his childhood. Falling in love with literary arts at a young age, Gage enjoyed spilling his imagination onto paper whenever he had the chance. Due to unfortunate events, he had to move back to California where he was thrown a faster paced lifestyle. He is currently attending Crafton Hills College pursuing a career in Radiology.

The One with the Christmas Party

Ayden Kelly

"A Friend" by Gillian Jones

A person who will listen and not condemn

Someone on whom you can depend

They will not flee when bad times are here

Instead they will be there to lend an ear

They will think of ways to make you smile

So you can be happy for a while

When times are good and happy there after

They will be there to share the laughter

Do not forget your friends at all

For they pick you up when you fall

Do not expect to just take and hold

Give friendship back, it is pure gold.

A Christmas party probably was not the best idea, considering final due dates and exams were just around the corner ready to pounce. For the past few weeks, students had been scrambling to either miraculously bring their grades up or hold on to the last bit of strength long enough not to let them slip. It was like the equivalent of hitting the last lap in Mario Kart, and once the music sped up, the pressure to stay anywhere above third place or pass up a few people was on. A tired metaphor, yes, but it still applied.

For Alena Perez, she had done all she could do as far as preparing for finals went. She had stayed on top of her homework, completed the study guides, and put in at least an hour or two of review time for each class on days when she was not working. Tomorrow was her first day of finals, the day of reckoning. Okay, maybe she was being a tad bit dramatic. Alena knew she was ready to ace those exams, but she was also realistic, so she was ready to get a C- or better. Now, it was time to unwind a bit before finals, and tonight was the night that she and her friends from work had agreed should be the one on which they would have their Christmas party.

Her parents were visiting family out of state anyway and were perfectly fine with allowing her to have people over. A nice little get-together for Alena and her friends was exactly what they needed too, not to mention well-deserved, after the grueling semester some of them had. Nothing fancy, just spending time together and laughing over dinner, dessert, and opening up presents from the Secret-Santa gift exchange. Alena just hoped no one would cancel because she had already cleaned up her house, and a few hours of hanging out would not kill anyone. No one had canceled so far, so she finished mopping in peace until she heard the doorbell ring.

"Merry Christmas!" an impossibly cheerful voice declared as someone swung the door open. Stepping into the house, with a beautifully wrapped box tucked underneath one arm and a gift bag in the other, was Alena's good friend Jazmin from work and school. "Oh, wow! When you said you were gonna clean your house, you meant *clean* clean."

"Well, it's been a while, so might as well," Alena said with a shrug as she glanced around the living room that was still a little wet from when she had mopped. "Where's Evelyn? I thought you guys were coming together."

"We did," Jazmin began, moving to the kitchen/dining room and setting her stuff on the table. "We've got a few things in her car that we still gotta get."

"Oh, hold on!" Alena exclaimed, making a quick trip to her room to grab her shoes, which she put on only halfway before jogging awkwardly back to where Jazmin was standing. "Let me help."

Both girls made their way to Evelyn's car that was parked at the curb in front of the house. Alena greeted her as they got closer. Inside Evelyn's trunk were several grocery bags containing frozen fettuccini, a sandwich platter, a couple of bags of chips, a box of those heavenly sugar cookies, a few bottles of soda, and a delicious-looking apple pie.

"Aww, guys. You didn't have to do all this," Alena said in surprise, snatching up a bag in each hand. "You guys didn't spend too much did you?"

Evelyn waved her hand dismissively. "Don't worry about it, dude. Everyone decided to pitch in for the food and stuff."

"Not you, you're hosting," Jazmin interjected, holding a hand up before their friend could protest.

The three of them carried the groceries inside. Evelyn and Jazmin emptied out the contents onto the breakfast bar while Alena set the oven on 'bake' for the fettuccini. Once that was done, Evelyn was left in charge of watching the oven, so she got to work putting out the rest of the food. Meanwhile, the other two girls continued tidying up the house, but Alena had finished with most of the cleaning and tidying up anyway, so they just lit some candles around the living room, kitchen, and bathroom. Jazmin eagerly switched on the lights to the Christmas tree, bouncing gleefully on the balls of her feet as she stepped back to look at it fully. Shaking her head and chuckling lightly to herself, Alena connected her laptop to the TV through airplay, filling the house with the jazzy melodies from Vince Guaraldi's *A Charlie Brown Christmas* album.

"We are ready," Alena whispered dramatically, and as if on cue, the doorbell rang.

"I got it!" Jazmin announced, making her way to the door and opening it to reveal Eva, Emilie, and Jayne standing on the other side.

"Hello, hello!" Alena sang, pushing herself off the couch to greet her friends.

"Hey, guys!" Emilie said loud enough for them all to hear before presenting Alena with a square glass container. "My mom made leche flan for us all. She made it in the way they do in the Philippines, so I hope you guys like it."

"I honestly don't think it is too different from the Mexican version," Jayne threw in. "I think my mom said the Filipino version has egg yolks and then it is also steamed, but that's pretty much it."

"Oh, well, either way it looks great, so tell her thank you." Alena smiled brightly and took the dish from Emilie to place it with the others, leading them all into the kitchen. "Go ahead and sit down. Are Diego and Johnny almost here?"

"Johnny just texted me and told me they finished closing up at work, so they should be on their way," Eva replied, setting her purse and coat on the chair by the entrance of the living room and then placing the gift she had brought underneath the tree as the other girls had done.

"They'd better be. I'm Johnny's Secret Santa," Jayne threatened jokingly.

Emilie let out a slight snort. "I like how this whole thing started as a Secret Santa, but then we all told each other whom we had, and then we eventually just connected the dots."

"Except Diego, he didn't tell anybody who he had," Eva added, shaking her head at how pointless his secrecy had ultimately been.

"Dude, me and Alena threatened to sit on him if he didn't tell us who he had," Evelyn said, moving around the breakfast bar to join in on the conversation at the table. Emilie, Eva, and Jazmin had already taken the chairs closest to the wall while Jayne sat at the head, so she plopped in the middle chair on Alena's right, which left the ones on Evelyn's right and the one at the end available for the boys.

Jazmin spoke then. She tinged slightly red from giggling at what she was about to say. "Imagine customers coming to the shop all ready to pay, and they just see a couple of Chicanas sitting on their manager screaming, 'Tell us who you got for Secret Santa!'"

"He would so fire you guys," Jayne chuckled. "But, I think he has Alena, because she has me, I have Johnny, Johnny has Emilie, Emilie has Jazmin, Jazmin has Eva, Eva has Evelyn, and Evelyn has Diego, which leaves Alena."

"You should be a detective," Emilie mumbled, reaching over to pat Jayne's shoulder, causing a round of laughter.

The noise ceased when Evelyn perked up upon seeing the porch light flicker on through the window. "They're here! Thank the Lord. I'm starting to get hungry."

Everyone cheered softly, partly because they were happy to see all the coworkers together, but mostly because they wanted to eat. The food smelled amazing too, especially when Evelyn took out the aluminum tray of baked fettuccine from the oven, steam emitting from it once she took off the cover. Johnny and Diego were forced to go first because they had just clocked out of work, but being the gentlemen they were, the boys insisted one of them go instead. In the midst of them trying to be polite, Evelyn eventually groaned loudly and pushed passed them all.

"You guys are taking too long," Evelyn mumbled, unashamedly serving herself.

"See, Evelyn's the only one that listened," Diego said, receiving a thumbs up from the girl in response.

"Gosh, Diego. We were just trying to be nice," Jazmin snipped in a silly valley-girl voice as she took her turn.

"Oye, soy sólo digo," he muttered, holding his hands up defensively.

"He tries to seem nice to hide the fact that he's the devil in disguise," Johnny whispered to Jazmin conspiratorially.

"You're the devil in disguise," Alena began to sing in her best Elvis impression, "Oh, yes you are the devil in disguise."

"That was amazing," Jazmin deadpanned, biting back a smile.

The others continued serving themselves, keeping the conversation lively and playful with the occasional witty banter, even a few occasional jabs. It was all in good fun, of course. They had grown close enough over the time they had spent together to be at the sort of level with each other. Together, they could crack jokes and share a few laughs, even at the face-palm inducing ones that caused secondhand embarrassment. Each of them were allowed to freely make fools of themselves and say something completely ridiculous without any serious judgment, but that didn't mean no one got teased.

"Wow, Diego. We can't take you anywhere." Jayne shook her head in mock disappointment but was clearly stifling a laugh.

Diego, still red-faced, was wiping up the area of the table where soda had sprayed from his mouth after hearing something hilarious Jazmin had said. "I'm sorry," he managed to say, "I wasn't expecting that.

While everyone else was watching Diego fail at life, Alena happened to notice something was off about Eva. She was smiling along with everyone else, yet the look in her eyes suggested she was preoccupied,

"You okay, Eva?" Alena inquired delicately while also trying to appear casual as not to bring any unwanted attention to her if it was not necessary.

Eva shook her head, although it was not very convincing. "No, I'm good."

Johnny was watching her, too. "You worried about finals?"

"No, no, I'm actually feeling pretty confident about tomorrow." Eva nodded her head, wearing an expression that was simultaneously certain and hesitant for some reason.

"What's up then?" Emilie asked softly.

Now everybody's attention was focused on her. Some had even stopped eating, which made Alena wince a bit because she was trying to avoid putting her friend on the spot, but if something were truly bothering her, then it was best for Eva to get it out now.

"I don't know. It's just..." Eva sighed heavily, pursing her lips thoughtfully. "I guess I'm feeling sort of disappointed with where I'm at, you know? Like Christmas is next week, and it's almost the New Year, yet here I am still working in the mall, living paycheck to paycheck, and still trying to put myself through school. Last semester, I was hoping to finally transfer to a four-year this fall, but I recently found out they don't offer two of the classes I really need, so I had to change my major. Now, I'm looking at another year at the community college, even though I have more than enough credits to transfer, but I'm pretty much stuck there." Eva sucked in a deep, calming breath upon realizing she was venting, and then raised her cup of soda with a grin. "Now that I've ruined the mood, Merry Christmas everybody!"

There was a small round of chuckling, and some of the seriousness in the atmosphere seemed to ease a bit before Eva continued. "I'm sorry. I didn't mean to, like, ruin the mood. It just sucks, you know? I was so close to moving forward, but I ended up getting pushed back."

All of them made noises of understanding, but Jazmin actually spoke up. "No, dude. We all understand what you're going through. I was at Cal Baptist when I first started working with you guys, but then my financial aid couldn't help me cover the cost of a private school or even a public one, so I had to go to a junior college like you guys."

"That sucks, dude," Evelyn said, wrinkling her nose empathetically. "You went from going to a top-rated school to whatever you want to call that place we go to now."

Jazmin shrugged nonchalantly. "I mean, there's nothing wrong with going to a junior college. Plenty of people go because it's cheaper and makes going to a four-year easier. Sure, I would've preferred to go to a better school, but I'll get there eventually."

"That's what I keep trying to tell myself," Eva mumbled, shoving another forkful of food into her mouth. "But it's hard to believe that when some of my other friends are starting to get real jobs, getting married, and having kids. Actually, the last part I don't have a problem with. I don't really plan of having kids until my late twenties, maybe my early thirties."

"Seeing all that makes you want it, though," Jayne chimed in as she got up to throw her plate away, graciously offering to take the ones of whoever else was finished. "I think we all wish we were at that point in our lives where we finally get to settle down and we have jobs we actually enjoy. No offense, Diego, we love working for you."

Diego offered up a smile as she sat back down, while Johnny clapped him on the shoulder. "No, no, I don't blame any of you guys. I'm a manager. That's cool, but I'm the manager at a coffee shop, not a multimillion-dollar company or anything."

"You're a manager at a multimillion-dollar company in our hearts," Jazmin cooed, patting Diego's arm affectionately.

"What?!" he squeaked, his eyebrows furrowing in confusion. Jazmin merely guffawed and shrugged because she didn't really have an answer for him.

"Okay, but Jayne makes a good point," Alena said, continuing the conversation. "We're seeing some people our age, not a lot, but we're still seeing some kids making a really good living. Like Angelo and Jessica." She turned to Evelyn, "Remember, we saw them pass by work the other day, and we started talking about how done we are with school and how we just wanted to get on with our lives?"

"Oh, yeah." Evelyn nodded, recalling the conversation she was referring to. Jessica and Angelo were their former managers who had left after getting a chance to pursue their dream careers. They had all been so happy for them but were sad to see them leave. "Those two actually have their lives together."

"Oh, my gosh! I was thinking the same thing!" Emilie gushed, flapping her hand in Evelyn's direction. "Like, they're our age, but they're already finished with school and everything.

"I feel like that's so rare nowadays," Johnny added. "Most people can't even go straight to a four-year and graduate in the time it took Angelo and Jessica, and they did it by the time he was twenty-three and she was twenty-one."

"True," Alena muttered with a nod. "Took my brother seven years just to get his BA, and it took my sister six. School is a lot more competitive now- and expensive."

Everyone groaned, knowing from experience the toll of college expenses has taken on them financially. If they listened closely, they would probably hear each of their bank accounts grumbling the way empty stomachs do.

"Honestly," Alena began, pacing her elbows on top of the table, "even though I know these next few years are going to be so rough for us, at least we can proudly say that we got through it. Once we all have stable jobs, a good income, no stress, and a place to call our own, we can look at all of it knowing we earned it and that we deserve it. You know what I mean?"

They all looked so wistful and hopeful, as if they were imagining it as Alena spoke. That life was so close yet seemed so far, but based on the looks they exchanged, they were confident it would happen for them. Eva, however, seemed to have a much different future for herself in mind.

"And when that happens, we can all have dinner at my mansion," Eva chirped with a flip of her dark hair.

"Really, you're complaining about being broke, but you want a mansion?" Evelyn drawled out with a tiny snort.

"Yup," Eva replied, popping on the 'p.'

"Hey, she lives a champagne lifestyle on a lemonade budget," Alena murmured with a snort, standing up while the others were laughing. "Alright, y'all. Who's ready for dessert and presents?"

Their eager replies were accompanied by the sound of chairs scraping against the floor and the low murmurs of side conversations sprouting. Alena took out a knife and cake server spatula, handing them to Jazmin, so she could cut the pies and flan, before moving over to prepare and set the coffee maker. By the time every person had received a plate, moved to the living room and chosen a spot to sit, the entire house was filled with the sweet aroma of fresh coffee. Eva was the first to jump up when she heard the beep, announcing it was ready.

Presents were distributed once the gang was situated. Jazmin, Eva, Jayne, and Emilie all sat comfortably on the larger couch; Evelyn and Alena on the loveseat; and Diego and Johnny in the two chairs on the other end. Partially empty mugs and paper plates were scattered on top of the coffee table, and tissue paper and torn wrapping paper were being thrown across the room and into a trash bag that had been brought out. Johnny and Diego had turned it into a competition, though.

In the midst of all the laughter and smiles that brightened the room, Alena couldn't help but notice that the scene before her resembled what she had imagined her future looking like: all of her friends in her living room, except at the home that she hoped to someday own. Her house or apartment would be cozy and inviting. It would, preferably, be raining outside, and they would all be laughing, with no stress.

Someday, it would happen, for all of them.

About the Author

Ayden Kelly is currently a student at Riverside Community College. His love and interest in writing began at a young age, which ultimately led him to pursue a major in English and Literature. The short story, "The One with the Christmas Party," was partly inspired by Ayden's friends as well as the experiences they faced and dealt with together. It was important to him to write a story that people, especially young adults, could relate to and, hopefully, feel uplifted as they read. The title of the story is also a reference to the famous sitcom *Friends*, which had episode titles that often began with "The One (With/Where)…"

A Christmas Without Her

Laura Loubriel

"A twin is a soulmate connected at the heart for life."

Unknown

I could not wait to go to Georgia, but the way there would not be easy. I had been waiting all summer to see my sisters and niece who I have had to watch grow up over a screen. I woke up early at 4am on August 1 and got dressed in the comfortable clothes I chose the day before and packed my bags in the car. My mother and I were off on the highway without thinking that we didn't have much to eat. I had only eaten a bagel and drank some water.

Traffic was unpleasant to say the least. Drivers cut us off every chance they got. When we arrived to the rental place, let's just say it was busy and hot. Riding the bus to the airport was a quiet and warm ride not to mention bumpy, but I put all that out of my mind. I was too excited. When we arrived at the airport, we got in line to send our baggage through. Afterwards was the wait for my mother's wheelchair. Believe me when I say it took half an hour for the chair and the person to arrive. Her excuse was, "Oh, I wanted to come get you when it was closer to your boarding time." That did not put me at ease. I'm the person who doesn't like airports because it stresses me so much with the checking and the walking and all the procedures, but I understand they are there for a reason.

So, as we were walking through everything, I could barely keep up for two reasons. One, I'm a very short person, according to society standards. 5'0 is considered short, and I'm 4'11. Two, I was carrying a very full backpack plus my mom's purse, while trying to keep up with the worker. After the trek across a big airport, I finally turned to my mom and said, "Let's get something to eat." So, we went to search for food in a crowded shop. Now, if walking across the airport didn't work up a sweat, just standing in the shop definitely did. It was packed.

After getting food, we ate, and I told my mom, "Hey, mom. I need to get gum and some pain medication," because as always, my period comes at the worst time. So, there I was two hours until I left for Atlanta. I was just so happy but so tired at the same time because of the fact I could not and did not sleep at all from excitement. So, I texted my friends and my sister and listened to music, when out of nowhere I felt I tap on my shoulder. It was a little boy who was going on a plane for the first time. Remembering the first time I went on a plane, I decided to settle some of his nerves.

After talking for a while, he had to board the plane to New York. Wishing him the best luck, I went back to my music until it was time for boarding. The advantage of having a disabled parent who can't walk in airports is you board first, meaning you don't have to deal with the chaos that ensues on planes when boarding.

Ten minutes later, everyone was seated, and we started to take off. I could not for the life of me figure out why I hate takeoff. My sisters always tell me it is stupid to get nervous at takeoff, but I was so calm that time because for one, I was very excited about seeing my sisters in three to four hours. Two, I visualized myself in a field so calm and peaceful. Three, the most important thing was I had the Lord with me. Believe me, I prayed before and during takeoff; I had faith.

So, we took off smoothly. I relaxed and with all the visualizing, I fell asleep. Thank the Lord. One hour later, "ding" went the seatbelt sign, and people began talking and moving, waking me up. My mom, of course, was asleep. So, I played games on my phone and decided not to be stupid and waste my battery as my inner voice was telling me. I spent the remainder of the flight staring at the clouds. I was in love with the view. It was hands down always my favorite part of flying. It was like I was a marshmallow surrounded by white fluffiness.

Soon enough, we were landing in Georgia, and I stared at my phone, waiting to see the time change. Let me tell you about the landing. My heart was beating out of my chest, and it wasn't because I was excited. It was because I thought I was going to die that day, and I was so close to seeing my sisters. The landing was extremely bumpy, and that wasn't the first time during the flight. There was so much turbulence that I was close to crying. Everything was shaking and quaking, and it didn't help that a woman in the back decided to yell, "Hell, yeah! This is my town finally," along with more sayings after that.

Getting off the plane, I was ready to kiss the ground. There I was walking through the airport thinking, *Wow, it's so big.* Then, to my surprise, there was a subway in the airport. Then, me being me, I almost fell twice, but I balanced myself until we got to an elevator to take us to the baggage claim. We waited probably twelve minutes for our bags. Going outside, I was texting my twin; we were minutes from each other. I couldn't wait to see her in person again. Then, my mom, at the last minute, said to me, "Don't act crazy." Slightly offended, I put that out of my mind, for it was seconds before seeing them.

Then, my sister sent a text saying, "Look for the car blasting Hamilton." So, I expected to hear Hamilton. Eventually finding them, I put the heavy bags in the truck, and I got in the car. When I came face-to-face with my sister, I didn't freak out. Even I was surprised, but it was like we went on as though we hadn't been separated for a year. I finally saw my three-year-old niece in person. I was speechless; she was so precious. She was so happy to see me that she asked to hold my hand on the way to dinner.

As we arrived to *Steak and Shake,* she said, "I want Lulu to carry me." Believe me when I say for such a small thing she was very heavy. Seated and looking over the menus, our waiter came and introduced himself with the most unexpected name. "Hello, my name is Cheeto, and I shall be your server today." And, we had a pleasant meal. Our next stop was every child's favorite place: Toys 'R Us. We roamed the aisles and played on bikes and scooters. By the end of our time at the store, we had bought my niece a baby dinosaur to hatch.

Pulling into my sister's neighborhood, I was tired but didn't expect the tilt of her driveway. I took the bags inside, and two minutes later, my niece accidently hit me with a metal pail. Let's just say the dogs missed me, particularly my twin's dog Sam; he's a softie.

Later, I took everything upstairs, and I found myself in my twin's room. It was very nice. By the end of the night, I had been caught up in her school projects and how she was her teacher's favorite. I myself was beyond proud of my brilliant twin and so happy to see my big sister. The next morning, I woke up alone and went downstairs to find my niece watching Nick Jr. We spent the morning watching TV and bonding. Afternoon rolled around, and I had to change because I had to go around Georgia in an Uber because someone had to go the ER with my mom. After a quick trip to the hospital, my sister picked us up, and we went to Kmart, where we went grocery shopping.

The next day, I wondered how the heck my sister gets up so early and quickly. I went downstairs to my niece who was running towards me to watch cartoons with the dogs beside us. My sister Alisa and I spent the day on the couch watching TLC shows and eating pizza. By the third day, I still didn't get how to wake up early toddler time, but that day I did find out how committed my niece is to dress up.

I had been saved from Sam the doggy dragon by a fearless pirate, and that also was the first time I gave my niece a bath on my own. As much fun as that was, I still had a lot to learn about being an aunt. Unfortunately for me, my sisters were watching the YouTube Pimple Popper, which led to having my face dissected by my sisters. Nevertheless, my face looked nice the next day.

The fourth day, I woke up an hour after my niece and sister. I woke up to something I had been looking forward to: my big sister making breakfast. She made the best food in my opinion. After breakfast, everyone showered, and we went to the mall. We walked around for a while until we came upon an eyebrow place, where I was convinced to get mine done. Tasia had said, "Forget the person who hurt you," as she referred to the woman who did mine back in Redlands. By the end, it was less painful, and the woman did a good job.

Afterwards, we decided to go to Medieval Times because none of us had been. As we looked around waiting for the show to start, I was looking at crowns with my niece when out of nowhere a loud noise rang, scaring both of us. We immediately hugged each other. At that moment, I felt so happy that the little girl was my niece, and I was so lucky to be her aunt.

About the Author

Laura M. Loubriel was born a preemie twin at the end of the 20th Century. She is a Hispanic artist, blending into her soul two great cultures: Mexican and Puerto Rican. It is just a treat to have conversations with Laura and enjoy her knowledge of books, writers, and series for avid readers on fiction stories. She enjoys reading, creating art, sewing, fashion design, music, and history. Laura enjoys nature walks, traveling, and watching the starry nights. Writing comes natural to her, and she likes writing about life and real events.

Merry Christmas!

Christmas Memories

Alyson Martinez

"She is clothed in strength and dignity and laughs

without fear of the future."

Proverbs 31:25 (NLT)

As far back as I can remember, the Christmas holiday was hard for me and my siblings. In 1982, at the age of six, my dad was involved in a horrific car accident that changed our lives forever. My sister was three, and my mom was pregnant with my brother. We lived in a nice apartment in Moorpark, CA. My dad's accident left him severely crippled. He lost the use of his entire right side and the ability to speak or even use the bathroom on his own. He required all of my mother's attention. I remember very vividly the day we got the call about my dad and the pain that was written all over my mom's face. At the young age of six, my roles as daughter and sister changed. They took on a whole new meaning. I became the second mom to my brother and sister.

We went from having what we needed to having almost nothing at all. We eventually had to move. My mom couldn't do it by herself anymore. She needed help, and the only place we had to go was to my grandma's house in Muscoy, a small city in San Bernardino, CA. My mom struggled to take care of us financially and was emotionally drained. I could see it written all over her face, even though she tried not to show it.

Eventually, we were able to rent a small house with two bedrooms and one bathroom, on June Street, a few doors up from my grandma's house. The kitchen was an ugly lime green color. It had a small dining room attached to the living room, right off the kitchen. The house was small and was owned by Ms. Zimmerman, a crazy old lady who lived next door. It didn't matter how big or small the house was, we were just happy that my dad was alive and we were all together. However, the struggle was just beginning.

My mom and I had to teach my dad how to walk, talk, and use the bathroom, along with everyday living. He suffered from extreme seizures that were so scary, especially for my brother and sister. Our lives were consumed with his care; it was a lot of work, physically and emotionally. By that time, years had passed, and my dad's recovery, according to doctors, was going to take a lifetime. He would never be the same. Even though my mom knew her life was going to be centered around my dad, she didn't mind, for he was the love of her life. Everyone told her to put him in a home, but she refused, always saying,

"I married him for better or for worse, and that doesn't change- no matter what." She knew the uphill battle she was facing and met it head on. She had all of us take classes to learn how to care for him. She put me and my siblings in counseling, to make sure we had some type of emotional support.

My brother was then starting kindergarten, my sister was going into the third grade, and I was going into the sixth grade. While my mom was taking care of my dad, I would get my brother, my sister, and myself ready for school. It was my responsibility to take care of them, even though it was never mentioned. I wasn't sat down and told what my new responsibilities where. I just stepped in and did what I knew I had to do. I knew they needed me. My childhood was gone at a very young age. I didn't get to do what the other kids my age were able to do. There were no sleepovers with my friends, and anytime I went to play with the other kids on our street, I had to take my brother and sister. I would look forward to going to school, to hang out with my friends, to play tetherball or do flips on the monkey bars. That was the only time I didn't have to worry about anyone else. It was my escape.

Holidays and birthdays were exceptionally hard. We didn't get big parties or lots of gifts. There was one Christmas I will never forget. I was in my last year of elementary school. We were going off on Christmas break, and I was so excited. We were going to get our Christmas tree after school. I ran to get my brother and sister from their classes. I remember the air was crisp, and the sky was a pretty shade of blue. As I zipped up my brother's jacket, I thought to myself, *I hope Mom got the tree. He will be so disappointed if she didn't.* Our walk home was about three country blocks that never seemed to end. We ran through the front door, and there it was: the biggest tree we had ever seen. It was so big that my mom had to take out the dining room table to make room for it. The tree made the house smell so wonderful. It was like walking into the forest.

The looks on my brother's and sister's faces were priceless. It was a look of pure happiness, something that we hadn't felt in a long time. That evening after my mom got back home from taking my dad to learning and development classes, she got out all the Christmas

90

decorations, and we spent time together decorating the tree. It was full of colorful lights, tinsel, and what seemed like a million bulbs. There were bulbs of every color: green, red, blue, and gold, to name a few. There were fancy bulbs and plain ones; some had glitter, and others looked like they were hand painted. When we were done, the tree looked so pretty. We were so proud of that tree.

Finally, Christmas Eve arrived! We couldn't wait to open that one special gift that we always got to open the night before Christmas day. As I carefully opened my present, I pulled back part of the wrapping paper and see a brown floppy ear. My heart jumped for joy. It was a brown pound puppy that I instantly named Molasses. Boy, did I love him. My brother got a big yellow Tonka truck, and my sister got a Barbie doll. We stayed up for a while and played with our new toys, excited about what the next day would bring. As my mom got my dad ready for bed, I tucked my brother and sister into bed and went to bed myself. I fell asleep thinking, *This is going to be a great Christmas.* At the same time, I worried that my mom had spent money on us that I knew we couldn't afford.

I woke up on Christmas day to the sound of my brother and sister yelling and laughing with excitement. Christmas was here! I ran to the living room to see my dad in his wheelchair, and my mom sitting on the floor beside my dad, next to the tree. I couldn't believe my eyes. There were so many presents. They filled the entire dining room, all round the tree. We got so many gifts. How can we afford this? How did my mom do it? It was a little overwhelming to say the least. It took almost the entire morning to open all the gifs. I remember getting redheaded, twin cabbage patch dolls that came with birth certificates, baby doll beds, and blankets. That was the absolute best Christmas ever!

About the Author

Alyson Martinez is very family oriented. She has six children and seven grandchildren whom she just adores. She has been married to the love of her life for almost twenty years. Alyson has accomplished many things. She has taught medical assisting and medical office admini-stration. She is certified to teach higher education and is a licensed phlebotomist. She is currently a graduate Employment Specialist at a career college and is working toward a BSN. Life has not been easy for her; however, the struggles she has faced made her the strong family and goal-oriented person she is today.

A Bloody Christmas

Mark Perez

"For life and death are one, even as the river and the sea are one."

Khalil Gibran

As the sun slowly crept up the horizon, shining its beautiful array of colors onto the snow-covered city, the people of the city began to wake up, getting ready for the last-minute Christmas shopping they seem to never avoid each year. The beams of light began to enter my room through the clear window in front of my bed, beaming and heating every inch of my face. I was beginning to awake. My eyes were opening and closing, trying to adjust to the bright light. Instead, it began to irritate my eyes. I decided to grab my blanket and put it over my head. The blankets many soft, warm fibers over my skin made me feel cozy. Getting out of my bed was the last thing on my mind. If it were up to me, I would stay home all day in my warm blankets, away from the bone-chilling weather outside.

Instead of doing that, I got ready for work, considering the fact that the day before Christmas is one of the busiest days of the year at Albertsons. Not showing up to work would be leaving my coworkers with less help for the crowds of people paying for their groceries. Upon opening the door to leave my house, a gush of cold wind crept up my sweater, pulling every pocket of heat I had left in my body. Goose-bumps instantly began to erect throughout my body, making me really pick up the pace to get inside my truck as soon as possible. Once I got inside my truck, I pulled out my keys from my pocket, putting one inside the ignition and turning it to start. My truck did not start, so I had to push on the gas pedal a few times for it to start. That wasn't a surprise to me because my truck was an old beat-up Chevy with rust patches scattered around its frost white paint.

Upon putting the truck in first gear and beginning to drive, I noticed that for this Christmas a majority of the city decorated their houses and front yards. In broad daylight, I could still see the many colors of lights that were hung on each house. Giant inflatable snowmen to tiny little reindeer were hung on doors. Every block I drove by gave me something to look at and admire. I decided to turn on my radio to hear some jolly Christmas music, but the music was suddenly interrupted by an emergency broadcast.

Immediately, the broadcast began by saying "This is not a drill. I repeat. This is not a drill. The public is to do the following: Remain in your homes for the next forty-eight hours. Wait for any help to arrive. Get as much rations that will last you and your family for about two weeks. There seems to be a pandemic of…" The radio on my truck shut off due to the circuit problems it had been having recently. Curiosity was really running through my mind as to what kind of pandemic was going on, even whether or not I should go to work that day. Pressing on, I made it into the parking lot of Albertsons and parked my truck in an open spot. I had been worried that I would not be able to find one.

Upon getting out of my truck, I could see the parking lot was very busy with at least a dozen people coming in and out of the grocery store. Elvin, one of my very close friends, was getting out of his car just across the parking lot. His face was filled with worry because the parking lot never gets filled to full capacity.

I yelled out his name, "Elvin!! Bro this is going to be a crazy day!" He turned around with a smile on his face, instead of the expression he had just a minute ago. We both went through a lot in that store; nevertheless, we overcame those problems. That was why we both felt more comfortable working our shifts, regardless of how busy it was.

Elvin replied, "Mark, this store is way over capacity, but hey you know what? It's alright. We will make it out of this."

I nodded my head and said, "You're right about that. By the way, did you hear on the radio about that pandemic going around?"

"No, I didn't hear anything about that. Are you sure you're not hearing things on the radio?" Elvin replied in a puzzled tone.

"Maybe I am going crazy and hearing things. There's just no way. But, all sounded so clear to me."

Elvin looked around the parking lot and said, "No, there's no way. Let's get inside, so we can clock in."

We both started walking towards the entrance of the store, where an enormous Christmas tree filled from top to bottom with shimmering, vivid decorations stood beside it. As soon as we walked in, most of the shelves were empty throughout the store. Every check stand was open and had a massive line of customers behind it, who were waiting to pay for their groceries. Three courtesy clerks we work with, Zavida, Alex and Dustin, were constantly yelling at customers to pay for the groceries they had in their carts, but they would not listen.

"What is going on, guys?" I asked the three. Dustin walked up to me and Elvin and said, "People are filling their carts and just leaving."

At that moment, I knew what I heard on the radio was not something deranged or a joke being pulled by the radio station.

Alex and Zevida began yelling, asking the man that just walked in "Are you okay, sir? What just happened?"

The man who walked in was very tall and slender with the right side of his body completely covered in blood. His eyes were black, and his skin was pale as snow. Elvin pointed out what seemed to be a bite mark on his neck. He looked straight at Alex, as if he was some sort of prey. Quickly, the man lunged straight at Alex, slamming him to the ground and beginning to chomp on his face and neck. Instantly, Alex began screaming, crying for help. What I was witnessing before my eyes was unbelievable. Every customer in the store began to run toward the two exits. Zavida quickly told all of the older employees by the check stands to get into the break room. The three of us did not have enough time because too many people were going in our direction, so we ran with the crowds of people out of the store.

As we began running, I could hear more people beginning to scream in agony. Turning behind me for one second, I could see Alex grabbing onto a woman, biting all over the old lady's body. His face was completely gnawed, and there were lacerations all over his body. The sight was so horrific I could not get the image out of my head.

When we reached the parking lot, Elvin said to me, "Let's all just go home and figure out what's going on right now."

Dustin and I responded by saying, "You've got a point. It's probably the safest place."

Getting inside of my truck, I put on my seatbelt, turned the truck on, and drove as fast as I could back home. Some of the roads were filled with traffic, so I avoided those roads at all costs. My mind could not fathom what I had just witnessed. Leaving to work on that day was a bad idea from the start I kept telling myself.

When I finally reached the block, I could see many of my neighbors with disturbed faces outside their houses on the phone with family members. Once parking my truck in the driveway, I ran to my door, unlocked it, and ran straight inside. Seeing the decorations in my home and feeling the warmth, really was a relief although throughout the rest of my day, I would hear the sirens ringing throughout the city, bringing me back to reality.

About the Author

Mark Perez was a Beaumont Fire Explorer for over four years, trained by many of Cal Fire's on-duty firefighters. He has dedicated many hours to provide volunteer work for the city of Beaumont through the Explorer Program. His educational background is a high school diploma earned at Beaumont High School, including a few certificates of completion from Hazmat Fro, Fire control seven, and Vehicle extrication classes. Additionally, Mark has completed two fire explorer academies: the IEFEA explorer and leadership academy, in the year 2017. Mark not only trained but worked part time for a year at an Albertsons in the city of Banning working as a checker and non-grocery clerk.

Merry Christmas!

Road Trip to Christmas

Karen Ruiz

VENI!

VINI!

AMARI!

(We came. We saw. We loved.)

Unknown

It was so magical, so tiring, full of every type of emotion you could possibly think of. At times, I didn't think my little nine-year-old body could handle so many emotions, but I was a trooper, and I stuck it out. Shoot, I didn't have any options. I was just nine years old and had no clue that there was a world outside my house. The fun started probably the first day of December.

I lived with my dad, mom, and two sisters. My oldest sister was named Daisy, and my youngest sister was named Kelly. Daisy was my dad's favorite kid, maybe because she was a spitting image of him and because she wasn't so girly like me. She preferred to run outside and play with the boys, instead of brushing her hair and painting her nails. She was thirteen and thought she was the toughest person and knew it all and made it her responsibility to look after Kelly and me. Kelly, on the other hand, was seven and a complete pain in the rear end. She got away with everything and was mommy's little girl. She did no wrong in Mom's eyes. In my eyes, she was the biggest crier and not the smartest cookie in the cookie box.

So, there we were. It was December 1st and only two weeks before winter break from school. Most importantly, the countdown to the biggest road trip we would take as a family. For three days and two nights, I would be stuck in the car with my dad's crazy driving, my mom's snoring, and my sisters arguing about who gets to sit where. Although the thought sucked, I was so excited to leave the country and spend Christmas with my family and get to experience my culture first hand.

Every day, for the next two weeks, when I came home, it felt like the living room kept getting smaller and smaller. Perhaps, it was because my mom made daily visits to Sam's Club and bought every-thing in sight to take to the motherland. I would ask her, "Ama, do we really need to take so many packages of water and snacks?" Her response was always, "Just you wait and see how blessed we are here and then complain." I just listened and kept counting down the days until we left for Mexico.

At last, the day had come. It was the last day of school before winter break, and that meant it was time to embark on the special road trip to Mexico. My dad finished piling up the Suburban with everything we needed and made sure the house was left decent. My sisters and I were ready to buckle up and go when five other trucks pulled up on our driveway. It caught me by surprise because inside those other five trucks were my aunts, uncles and cousins. We were all going to take the road trip together but obviously in separate cars. It was so exciting; it was almost like a huge game of follow the leader.

Off, we all went. First, we drove until the end of California; then, came Arizona; after was New Mexico; then, Texas. It felt like we drove forever once we reached Texas because we had to cross the border to get into Mexico. Then from there, it was about another twelve hours to reach our destination, which was Veracruz, Mexico. The nights were long, and the days were even longer. We sat in the car eating everything in sight and tried to drink as little water as we could, so we wouldn't have to make extra rest stops. We sang the same old songs over and over until we memorized every single lyric, while asking every five seconds, "Are we there yet?"

It wasn't until the third day of driving that we reached my grandma's house. The excitement was so unreal. I jumped out the car and ran to give my grandparents a big hug and kiss and to hug my cousins who lived with my grandparents. It felt amazing to be able to run around and to finally be reunited with my family. The drive was totally worth it because in that moment, everything was complete, and there were no worries in the world.

While the adults unloaded the cars, with our clothing and gifts for everyone, the kids ran, and just like in the Disney movie Ariel, I felt like it was a whole new world. The liberty we had of running around and discovering everything that was once nothing but a story told by my parents was awesome. There was a huge wishing well in the front of my grandma's house, and inside there was water. No one knew where it went, and we had to be careful about falling in. The lady next door sold fireworks, and anyone was able to buy them, for they were legal in Mexico. That was the first time I ever held a firework and ran so far to not get burnt.

On Christmas morning, there wasn't a Christmas tree set up, and there were not any gifts to exchange. That didn't matter though because it seemed so insignificant. In that split second, everyone in the room had a smile on their face and a full tummy. The gifts were each other's presence. Being able to travel across the country then out of the country to see family that I had not met before and being able to experience my culture was the best gift anyone could ask for. Being able to see how truly blessed I was to live in the United States and be healthy enough to travel back and forth was amazing. Even little nine-year-old me knew that was more than enough to ask for. That Christmas was one I will never forget.

Hearing stories from past Christmases from my grandparents and parents and being able to be surrounded by so much love and happiness and, most of all by family without the drama, was more than I could ever ask. I enjoyed the homemade tortillas and homemade hot chocolate, while being filled with stories that warmed my heart. Hearing all the traditions and laughing until my gut hurt from the crazy stories that were told by the elders was definitely the way to spend the holidays!

About the Author

Karen Ruiz is a small town girl with many hopes and dreams. Her family and friends call her Princess KareBear because of the way she carries herself and the way she loves others. Karen loves to travel and go on adventures. She's all about the memories and the breathtaking views the world has to offer. She is extremely dedicated and never takes no for an answer. She hopes to put her dedication and strong voice to help the youth by becoming a lawyer. She wouldn't be the person she is today if it wasn't for the love, support, and prayers from her mother Araceli, father Nahum Ruiz, and her two sisters Daisy and Kelly Ruiz. She lights up any room she walks into with her big smile and laughter.

It's Not a Perfect World

Dr. Cassundra White-Elliott

"Beauty in things exists merely in the mind

which contemplates them."

David Hume's Essays, *Moral and Political* (1742)

Once upon a time, in a land that never existed, in a secluded mansion, which sat at the top of a steep winding road, sat a thirty-nine year old woman, in the main parlor. The woman was no ordinary woman, not by any means. From the time she had been a teenager until her mid-30s, she had won beauty pageant after beauty pageant, and each win always came with a large sum of money. As a result, by the time she was thirty-six years old, she had become one of the wealthiest women in her local community, her state, and the neighboring states.

One evening, when the woman had been thirty-seven, her dedicated family chauffeur, of over twenty years, was driving her to one of the five-star restaurants in the downtown area, so she could meet her fiancé for dinner. As they made their way through the torrential rain, the woman began having second and third thoughts about traveling in such weather, even to see the love of her life, the man she would marry in just a few short months.

The woman was so absorbed in her thoughts that at first she was unaware that the tires of the car were skidding to the left, which caused the car to move into oncoming traffic. Before the woman realized what was occurring, the Lincoln town car in which she was riding, was sharply impacted by a Cadillac SUV. The Lincoln was fiercely pushed into the guard rail, and instead of the rail stopping the car's movement, the speed and the wet pavement caused the town car to flip over the rail and land in the ravine below.

The impact the town car received from the Cadillac caused the windows to shatter. Glass flew everywhere, including into the woman's face, leaving gashes on the right side. When the car landed in the ravine, the impact of the landing caused the car door to bend inward, jabbing the woman in her right leg, tearing her flesh open.

Feeling the jarring pain, the woman slowly began to lose consciousness. She tried fighting it, but her body was reacting to the severe pain she was experiencing, shutting itself down as a mode of preservation. In the distance, she could hear the wail of sirens and knew someone was coming to her rescue. Then, she heard her chauffeur's voice asking if she was okay. But, she could not answer, as she found herself shrouded in darkness.

When she finally came to, she was in a hospital bed, and twelve hours had passed. Shaking her head groggily, feeling the effects of the medication she had been administered, she looked around, attempting to detect her location. Before she could figure it out, she saw her fiancé sitting by the bedside. With a confused look on her face, she stared into his eyes. Noticing she was awake, he immediately began to explain what had transpired the night before during the storm, as she was making her way to meet him for dinner.

As he spoke, the woman felt something on the right side of her face. She reached up and felt a large bandage extending from the top of her cheekbone, under her eye, down to her chin. Then, she felt a sharp pain in her right leg. At that moment, the doctor walked into the room and introduced himself.

A few days later, the woman was released to go home. She was instructed to return to the hospital a few days afterward to have her wounds cleaned and her bandages replaced. After the first return hospital visit, the woman went once a week for the same treatment.

A few months later, the face bandage would be removed for the last time, and the woman would finally see the extent of her injuries. Up to that point, she had not wanted to view her face each time the nurse had offered.

Prior to going to the hospital that day, the woman had requested her fiancé's presence in the room for the unveiling. He quickly agreed to her request. He sat to her left side, holding her hand as the nurse carefully removed the bandage. Once the bandage was off, the nurse handed the woman a mirror.

Slowly, the woman lifted the mirror to her face, not really wanting to look, fearful of what she would see. As she lifted her eyes, she saw two horrors: the jagged scar that ran down her cheek and the horrified look on her fiancé's face, as he quickly rose from his chair. His abrupt change of positions, from being seated to standing, caused the chair to tip backward and hit the floor with a loud thud. He mumbled, "I'll be right back." He turned and walked quickly from the room, with his hand covering his mouth. It was as if he had suddenly grown nauseous.

A tear ran down the woman's face, as she once again lifted the mirror to her face. That time, she noticed for the first time that her right eye was drooping a little. While the bandage was on, she didn't much notice what was going on with the right side of her face. She just knew she had been in a lot of pain.

The nurse excused herself and said the doctor would be in a few moments. A few minutes later, the room to the door opened again, and the woman thought it was her fiancé returning. To her disappointment, it was only the doctor coming in. He sat down and explained the options of plastic surgery to repair the scar. However, he said it would be best to wait a few months until the inner tissue healed before any further surgery was performed. The woman, dumbfounded by her fiancé's reaction, wasn't really taking in what the doctor was saying because she was wondering what was keeping her fiancé. Why was he taking so long to return? After the doctor left the room, the woman sat patiently waiting for her fiancé. She was feeling numb and lost.

After a few moments of waiting and not getting an answer when she called his cell phone, she moved from the room to the waiting area for him to come and collect her and drive her back home. Unbeknownst to her, the moment she saw the back of his head leaving the room would be the last time she would see him in her presence. Finally admitting to herself that he was not planning to return or answer her calls, she called her driver to come and pick her up from the hospital.

As the woman sat in the family mansion all alone, as the last surviving member of her family, she decided to go into town. It would be the first time she did so after staying home for two and a half years since the accident. She had been thoroughly humiliated when she had read in the newspaper that her engagement to a well-known bachelor had been called off. He had not had the decency to tell her himself. She was heartbroken. From that point until now, she had everything ordered in and had only allowed a few close friends to come to her home.

But, on that December morning, two days before Christmas, after the snow had ceased falling for the past few days, she had made up in her mind that she would face her public, those who had once celebrated with her after each pageant in which she had been victorious. She decided she would not hide from the world any longer, and they could either accept her for who she was with the scar on her face or not. The choice would be completely theirs.

When the chauffeur pulled up outside the row of shops, the woman stepped out confidently with her head high. She was determined to go shopping to purchase a gift for the few friends who had not abandoned her and maybe a little something for herself. After being in the store for about thirty minutes, she heard a familiar voice call her name. Slowly lifting her head, the woman turned to face the man. To her surprise, it was an ex-boyfriend from college.

When he saw her face and the scar, he lifted his hand and caressed the side of her face and a tear ran down his face. The woman did not understand his emotion. She had not seen him for nearly fifteen years. She definitely did not want his pity. She attempted to step back, but he gently placed his hands on the tops of her arms and pulled her into him, embracing her.

"I have been trying to get in contact with you for years," he whispered into her ear. The woman did not respond. She did not know how to respond, so she remained silent while taking in his handsomely rugged good looks. He was still the same charming fellow he was all those years ago. That much she could tell.

"I read about the accident in the paper and the news about your engagement. I'm sorry about that. I was just so grateful to know you were okay and that you didn't marry that guy." She did not know how to take his comment. She didn't know whether she should take it personally or be flattered.

Finally, she spoke up and said, "Why were you trying to contact me?"

"I made the biggest mistake of my life when I broke up with you in college. I found that out a few years afterward. I wanted to reconnect with you."

"And now?" she questioned, as she lifted her hair from the side of her face, further exposing her scar.

"That doesn't concern me. I know the person inside. That is the person I fell in love with and have not been able to get out of my mind, even after marrying someone else."

"You're married?"

"Was. Not anymore." The man noticed a few of the other customers staring at them, so he pulled the woman into a quiet corner. "Look," he began, "give me a chance to show you that I'm not the jerk I once was." Thinking he may have been moving too fast, he asked, "Are you seeing anyone?"

With her head down, the woman said, "No," in a barely audible voice. The man placed his hand under her chin and lifted it.

"Have dinner with me tomorrow?" he asked.

"Tomorrow is Christmas Eve."

"Yes, I'm aware of that. Can we spend it together?"

With a smile on her face, the woman smiled for the first time in a very long time and responded, "Yes, that would be nice."

~~~~~~~~~~~~~~~~~~~~~

At the turn of the New Year, after having spent every day since Christmas Eve with her ex, who was then her current, the woman decided to have the plastic surgery. It wasn't because she felt compelled to. No, she would do it for her new fiancé. He had not asked her to, but she wanted to be beautiful for him, both inside and outside, on the day they would say their vows, even though he had accepted her as she was when he proposed to her on Christmas Day, not wanting to take the chance of losing her again.

She had accepted his proposal and scheduled the surgery a few weeks later. After she had healed completely, they would be joined together in holy matrimony, saying their vows before a few friends and family members. The woman could not be more overjoyed with the turn of events in her life. She had wondered how things would turn out after the turmoil she had suffered through with the changes in her body
~~~~~~~~~~~~~~~~~~~~~

and the loss of her first fiancé. She prayed for the best and truly believed in her heart that all would be well.

It just goes to show you that we don't live in a perfect world with perfect people with perfect actions. Life is what you make of it, and you must have the courage to live each day to the fullest, regardless of what the world around you thinks!

And, beauty is truly in the eyes of the beholder.

About the Editor/Publisher

Dr. Cassundra White-Elliott resides in California with her family, where as an English/Education professor she teaches at various community colleges and universities.

When writing, she writes with the direction of the Holy Spirit, in an effort to share with God's people all that He has for them.

In addition to teaching and writing, Dr. White-Elliott also serves as an evangelistic teacher. She is the founder of International Women's Commission, a ministry that serves the needs of the entire person, by attending to healing the mind, body, soul, and spirit.

Dr. White-Elliott holds a Ph.D. in Education, a Master's in English Composition, and a Bachelor's in Education.

Dr. White-Elliott is also the founder of CLF Publishing, LLC. For your publishing needs, go online to www.clfpublishing.org.

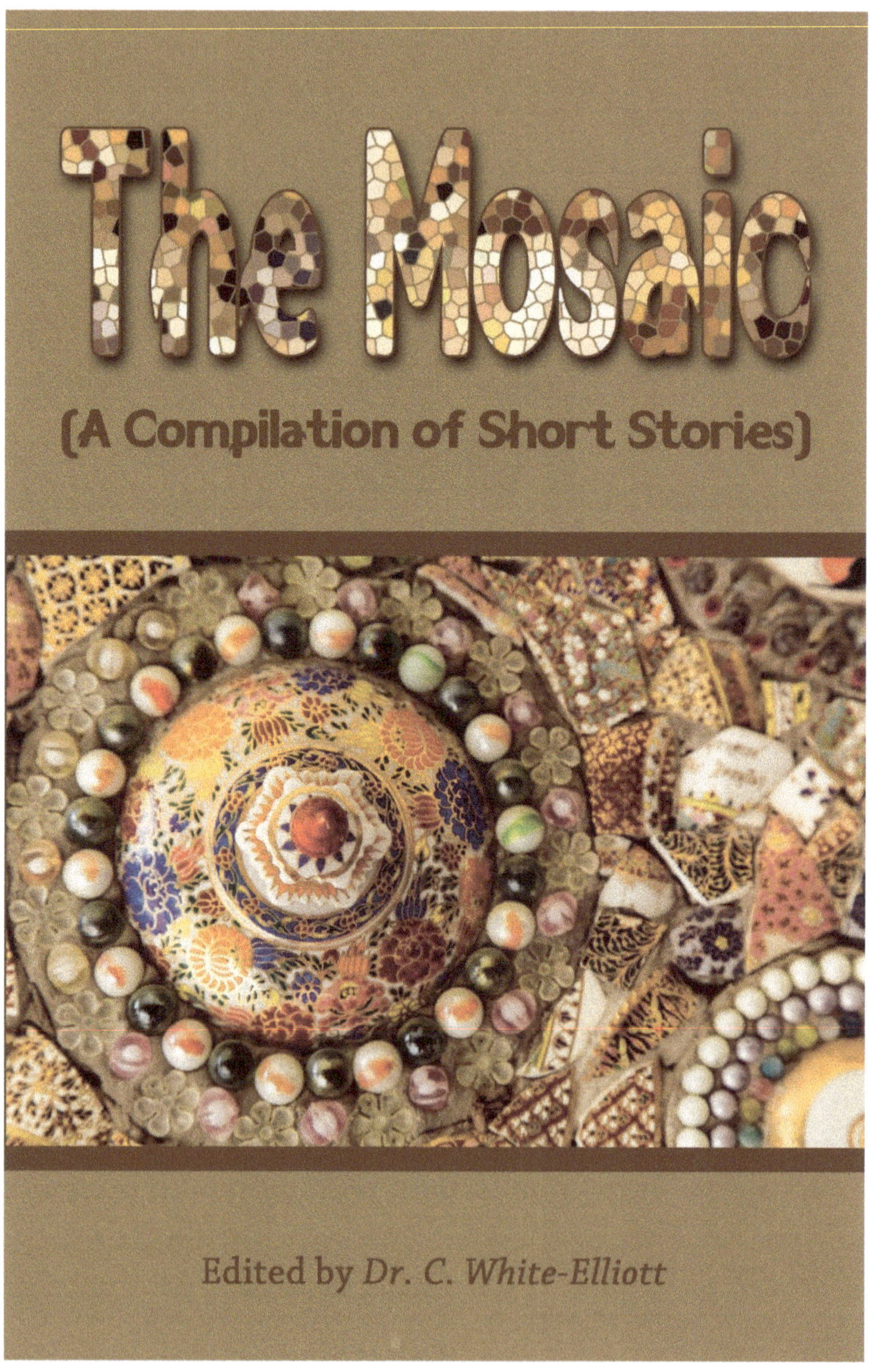
The Mosaic
(A Compilation of Short Stories)
Edited by Dr. C. White-Elliott

The Mosaic
(A Compilation of Short Stories)

The Mosaic is a collection of fourteen short stories written by fourteen different authors who wonderfully display their talent and their unique expression of creativity. The genres range from science fiction, to action, to suspense, to adventure, to fantasy, to drama.

Featured in this compilation are the following authors: Celine Acuna, Marissa Davisson, Kimberly Enriquez, Raena Fisk, Sandra Flores, Caroline Foster, Alexander Francisco, Mariah Halbert, Mone Makkawi, Stacey Ogden, Zak O'Mara, Jason Quezada, Kayghee Reynolds, and Gary Rodriguez.

sci-fi adventure action
fantasy drama fantasy suspense
eroticism action drama
suspense eroticism
adventure action sci-fi

CLF Publishing, LLC.
www.clfpublishing.org

www.creativemindsbookstore.com
www.amazon.com
www.barnesandnoble.com

The Mosaic II
Edited by Dr. C. White-Elliott

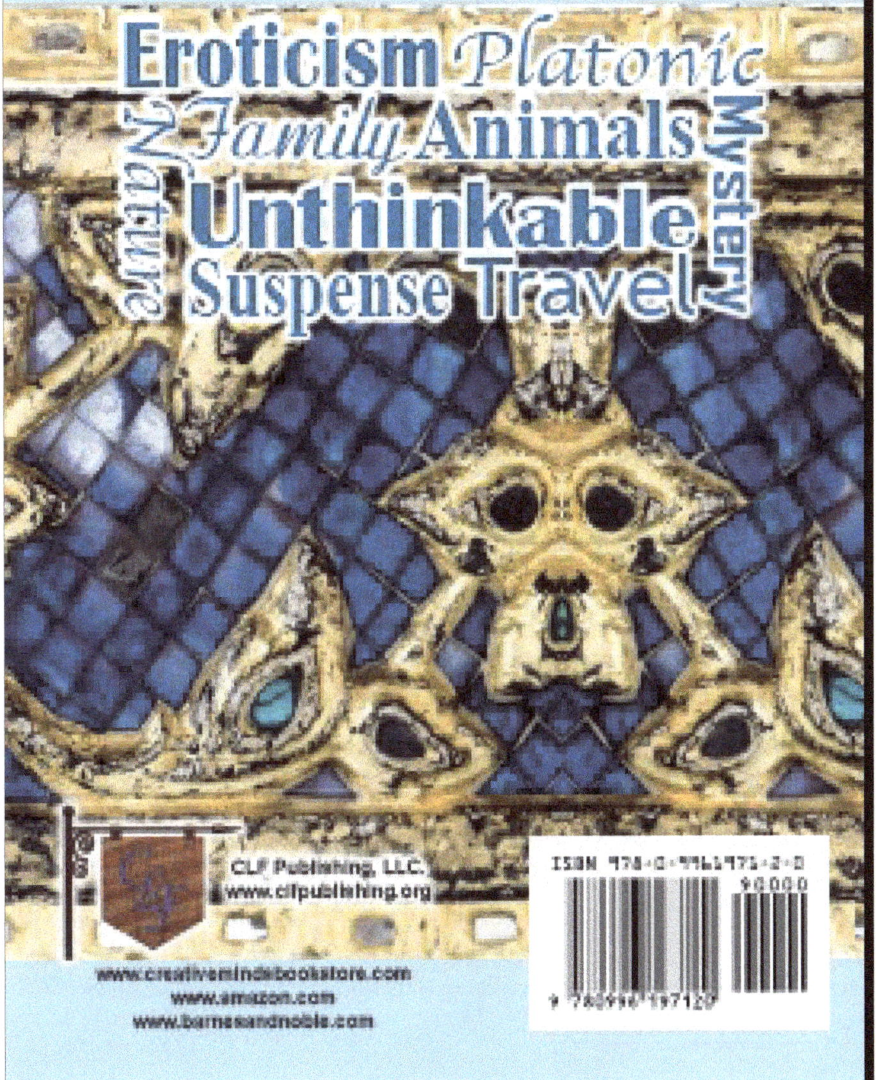
Take an adventure within the pages of The Mosaic II, where you will find stories filled with controversy, intrigue, mystery, amazement, and inspiration.

This compilation features the following authors: Samantha Blackwell, Tayani R. Davis, Kimberly Enriquez, Kathleen Hallo, Andy Halsig, Zak O'Mara, and Gary Rodriguez.

Eroticism Platonic
Nature Family Animals Mystery
Unthinkable
Suspense Travel

CLf Publishing, LLC.
www.clfpublishing.org

www.creativemindsbookstore.com
www.amazon.com
www.barnesandnoble.com

ISBN 978-0-9961975-2-0

The
Mosaic III
Edited by Dr. C. White-Elliott

Take an adventure within the pages of *The Mosaic III*, where you will find stories filled with controversy, intrigue, mystery, amazement, familial love, inspiration, and romance.

Eroticism *Platonic*
Nature *Family* **Animals** Mystery
Unthinkable
Suspense Travel

This compilation features the following authors:
Eliasar Astorga, Cindy Cazares, J. D. Delgado,
Danilo Escobar, Lorraine Faller, Noelle Gracia,
Haley Keil, Tyler Kowalski-Foley,
Johnathon Lopez, Iris Rangel,
Dr. C. White-Elliott, and Vanessa Zavala

CLF Publishing, LLC.
www.clfpublishing.org

www.creativemindsbookstore.com
www.amazon.com
www.barnesandnoble.com

ISBN 978-1-945102-04-2

THE MOSAIC IV
A Compilation
of Short Stories
Edited by
Dr. Cassundra White-Elliott

Take an adventure within the pages of **THE MOSAIC IV** (a compilation of short stories), where you will find stories filled with controversy, intrigue, mystery, amazement, family adventures, inspiration, science fiction, and romance.

This compilation features the following authors:
Krisha Mae Bacarro, Parker Balders,
Ruben Baltierra, Patricia Carrasco,
J.D. Delgado, Alicia Diaz, Danilo Escobar,
Don Franco, Jr., Kacey Fuentes,
Eli Giancanteri, Destiny Green, Erika Gudino,
Urooj Khan, Alicia Loredo, Alma Munguia,
Miguel Obregon, Karina Pedraza,
Tyler Rogers, Joshua Scott, Juliana Slaven,
Rodrigo Timis, Everardo Valenzuela,
Joselyn Violante, Wendy Waite, and
Guadalupe Zuniga.

www.creativemindsbookstore.com
www.amazon.com
www.barnesandnoble.com

THE Love Mosaic

Edited by *Dr. C. White-Elliott*

Love is universal and quite mysterious. It comes when you least expect it- like a thief in the night. It can bring joy, and it can bring pain. Love can have you one day up but the next day down; love can have you turning like a merry-go-round. Love goes where the heart takes it.

Love can be communicated and understood by a simple touch, a look, a kiss, or a hug. It can be communicated through a song, a poem, in a greeting card, and even through a love story. The story may have a happy ending- if all goes well. But that, of course, is not guaranteed. Before you know it, something can go unexpectedly wrong!

This compilation of love stories will have you on the edge of your seat. Some may bring joy to your heart, while others will cause you to shed a tear.

Each story shares love from a different vantage point. Some display love erotically, while others exhibit platonic love.

The stories included within this book bring love right to you in a manner you have never seen.

Featured in this compilation are the following authors: Katie Abbott, Samantha Blackwell, Michael Bril, Megan Duarte, Clarissa Flowers, Yadira Fuentes, Gavin Kenys, Karen Lopez, Stacey Ogden, Zak O'Mara, Danyelle Pappas, Kayghee Reynolds, Meagen Saiz, Daisy Sekly, Alexandria Stapleton, Haylee Vaughan, Jessica Yslas.

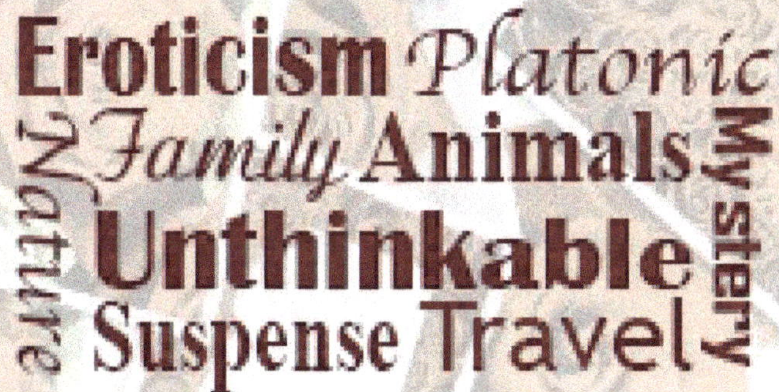

www.creativemindsbookstore.com
www.amazon.com
www.barnesandnoble.com

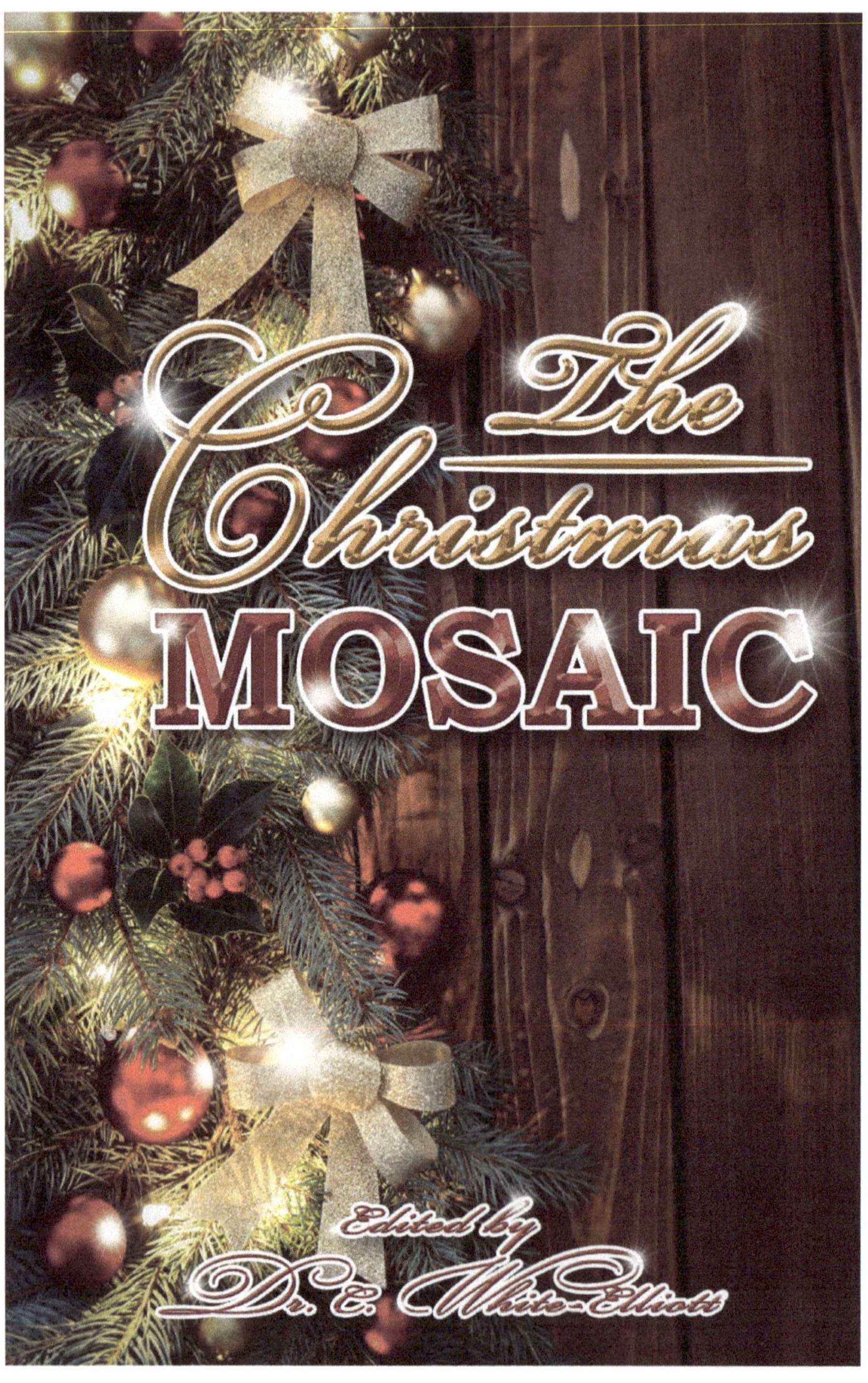
The
Christmas
MOSAIC
Edited by
Dr. C. White-Elliott

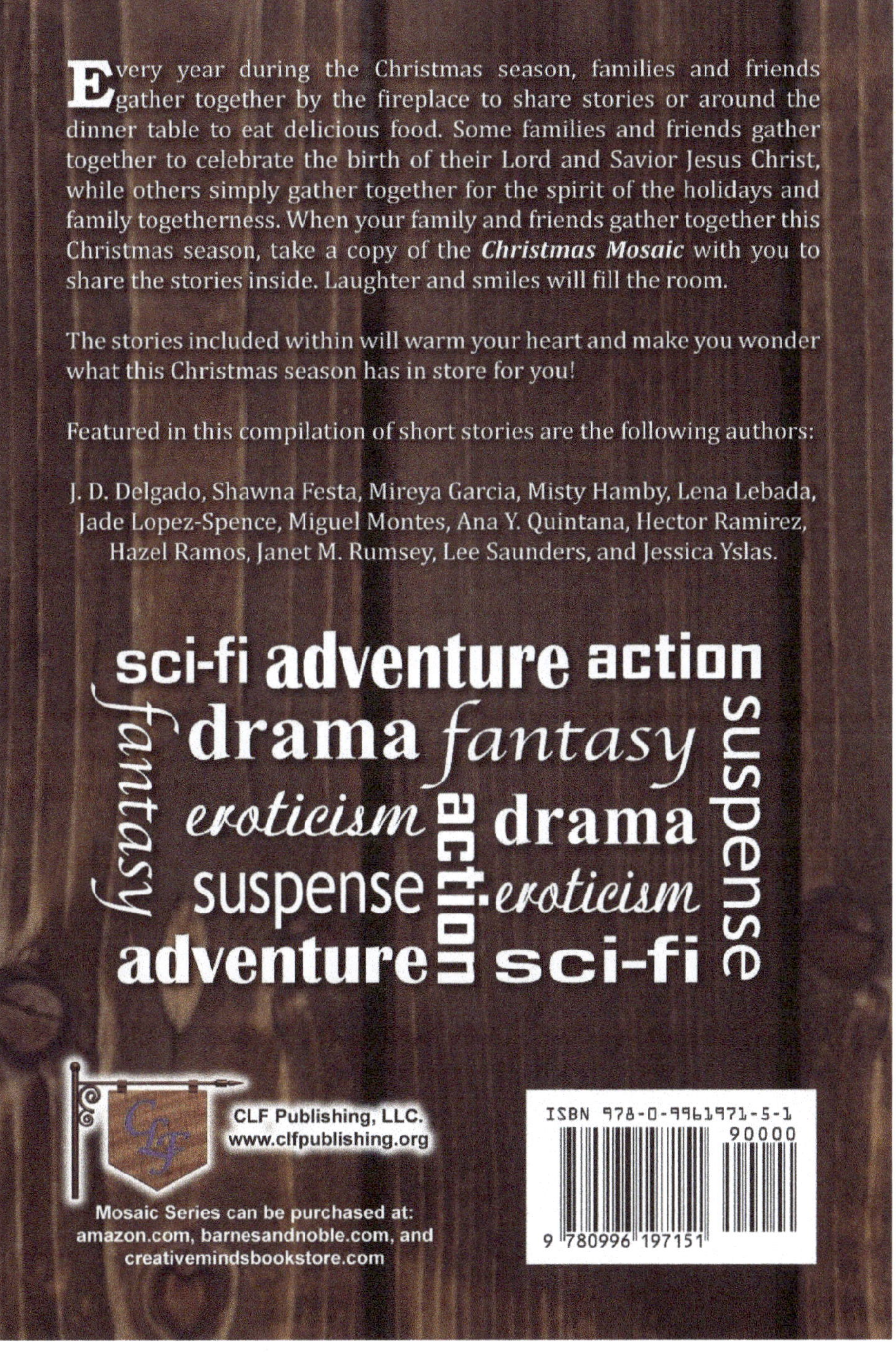

Every year during the Christmas season, families and friends gather together by the fireplace to share stories or around the dinner table to eat delicious food. Some families and friends gather together to celebrate the birth of their Lord and Savior Jesus Christ, while others simply gather together for the spirit of the holidays and family togetherness. When your family and friends gather together this Christmas season, take a copy of the **Christmas Mosaic** with you to share the stories inside. Laughter and smiles will fill the room.

The stories included within will warm your heart and make you wonder what this Christmas season has in store for you!

Featured in this compilation of short stories are the following authors:

J. D. Delgado, Shawna Festa, Mireya Garcia, Misty Hamby, Lena Lebada, Jade Lopez-Spence, Miguel Montes, Ana Y. Quintana, Hector Ramirez, Hazel Ramos, Janet M. Rumsey, Lee Saunders, and Jessica Yslas.

CLF Publishing, LLC.
www.clfpublishing.org

Mosaic Series can be purchased at:
amazon.com, barnesandnoble.com, and
creativemindsbookstore.com

ISBN 978-0-9961971-5-1